RUNAWAY GRIEVER

A Bereaved Father Runs Away From The Pain Of Grief

Dennis L. Apple

This is a work of fiction. The characters, incidents, and dialogues are products of the author's imagination and are not to be construed as real. Any resemblance to actual events or persons, living or dead, is entirely coincidental.

ACKNOWLEDGMENTS

I am deeply indebted to the following people who gave me the tools and encouragement to write this novel:

Harold Ivan Smith, my friend who first planted the seeds of writing in my mind.

Joni Woelfel, my tireless cheerleader. She believed in me when I nearly gave up on this project.

Peggi Johnson, Lora Krum, Jo Seitsinger, and Fatima Mcgarragle, all of whom are bereaved mothers who edited and encouraged me to keep writing. The great number of bereaved mothers and fathers I have met through The Compassionate Friends (TCF) support groups.

My wife and soul-mate, Buelah, who patiently stood by my side and gave me confidence to write this story.

Book club/small group questions included.

Also by Dennis L. Apple
"LIFE AFTER THE DEATH OF MY SON...
WHAT I'M LEARNING"

DEDICATION

In loving memory of our son, Denny 1972-1991.
In loving memory of my niece, Megan Riden 1983-1999
Jia's daughter.
In loving memory of my niece, Heather Rose, September 2005,
Scott & Terry's daughter.
In loving memory of my niece, Addison Kay Meyer, 2015, Joe &
Carly's daughter.
To our son Andrew and his beautiful wife, Amber,
of whom I am very proud.

"The Lord is nearest to the brokenhearted and saves those who are crushed in spirit."
Psalms 34:18

CHAPTER ONE

Charlie Davis was nearly 6 feet tall and weighed in at 175 pounds; a grown man. But at 48, everyone in his home town still labeled him JD's boy--the preacher's kid. When he was being honest with himself, Charlie admitted he sometimes still felt like a kid, especially in the presence of his dad, Reverend JD Davis.

Charlie had always dreaded Sundays. He grew up knowing he was expected--by his parents as well as the other churchgoers in Ladner, Missouri--to be in church for every one of his dad's sermons. He dreamed many times of moving somewhere else where he could live without the expectations that hung over his head, but he had never worked up the nerve to do it. JD was one of the most powerful men in town, and there weren't many people brave enough to cross him, including Charlie.

John Davis, who preferred to be known as JD, was an austere-looking man, taller than his son and 10 pounds lighter. His facial features were more pronounced than most 67-year-old men. His hairline was receding and his silver hair was parted down the middle and combed straight back. His wire-rimmed glasses were often off his face and in his left hand, especially when he was driving home an important point in one of his sermons. His bushy eyebrows and steely gray eyes reflected the silver of his hair. He favored dark suits for preaching but occasionally wore gray to appear even more distinguished. His countenance was stern, and he usually wore a frown or expression of deep concern. He used his boney fingers to punctuate his fiery sermons, and his index finger seemed a yard long when he pointed at certain folks in the congregation. His eyes flashed as he warned his flock of certain sins--especially those involving alcohol or sex. He preached with such passion and vivid description of hell that those sitting in the front half of the sanctuary declared they actually felt the temperature rising around them. Rumor had it that JD once ordered the air conditioning be adjusted to allow the temperature to rise by 10 degrees when he preached about hell. JD testified that he had experienced the threat of hell because he had been a devils' drunk for a good bit of his life, and he bragged that there had been a time there was nothing he wouldn't do when he got in the bottle.

This day, Charlie and his wife sat in their usual pew twelve rows back, piano side. Charlie daydreamed and only half listened as his father's sermon droned on. JD's sermons usually began with him announcing that he had three important points to make, but those three points often grew to a half dozen or more. Charlie always recognized when the sermon was drawing to a close, because JD usually ended with heart-rending stories of someone accepting Jesus as personal savior on the death bed or some other dramatic tale involving a serious accident.

JD's ending today described a horrible accident he had witnessed just three days prior. Charlie listened with full attention as JD stepped forward, took a deep breath, and with a serious whisper, said, "I came within a hair's breadth of going out into eternity just this past week!"

A hush fell over the sanctuary as nearly everyone leaned forward to hear the details. JD's story was wrapped in specifics.

"I was driving alone to Springfield to the Cox Hospital to see Sister Jenkins, who had a hysterectomy on Wednesday." Anna, JD's wife, sat on the front pew, and she knew where this story was going. She had hoped JD would leave out the details of Sister Jenkin's surgery.

JD took a deep breath. "The school bus in front of me was stopped with its red lights flashing and the yellow stop arm extended. Of course, I stopped right behind the bus." He paused and walked a little closer to the crowd who was hanging on every word. "Suddenly, I heard a loud horn right behind me and I *knew* it was not the horn of a car."

His voice raised to an excited pitch. "Looking in my rearview mirror, I thought my heart would stop as the front end of a bright red GMC 18-wheeler came full speed ahead straight at me!"

JD's loud, booming voice thundered on. "I cried out, 'Oh, God! I command, in the name of Jesus, stop that 18-wheeler from slaughtering these precious children--and me!'"

JD pulled off his glasses, took out his white handkerchief, wiped his eyes, and closed them. Eyeglasses in hand, he tilted his head toward the ceiling and solemnly whispered, "In those few seconds, my life flashed before my eyes, and I was certain I was going to die!"

Eyes still closed, a tear crossed his cheek. "I continued to pray. 'Lord Jesus, if you want to call me and these precious children home, we are ready to go.'"

Amens erupted across the congregation. They believed that if anyone was ready to meet the Lord, it was their pastor. Charlie had always known how his dad felt about children who were under what he called the age of accountability. If innocent children twelve and younger died, they would be taken home to heaven.

"As I watched in my mirror, a miracle took place right before my eyes!" Charlie's eyes swept across the faces of the folks seated close to him. No one moved. Even the teenagers stopped whispering among themselves and paid close attention, anticipating what had happened next. JD lifted his arm in a wide arch that helped the crowd see what he had seen.

"Something that looked like a white cloud, shaped like the giant arm of an angel seemed to come straight out of nowhere, straight down out of heaven! It was as though a powerful agent from God caused that truck to swerve to the right and into the ditch where it overturned and skidded for what must have been a hundred feet! A huge cloud of dust, rocks, and smoke sprayed in every direction!"

JD paused meaningfully while he waited as the scene sank into the consciousness of his listeners. His eyes were wide open now, and he stood fully in front of the pulpit and tearfully whispered, "I'm so glad I was paid up and prayed up."

The people nodded in amazement.

Again, this time a bit louder, "I'm *so* glad I was paid up and prayed up!" There was another scattered chorus of amens.

Not satisfied, JD clinched the microphone tightly and, just as he had seen popular television evangelists do, placed the microphone near his mouth and with fiery passion boomed, "I'M SO GLAD I WAS PAID UP AND PRAYED UP!"

A long explosion of amens and Hallelujahs echoed through the church! One of the few retired ministers in the congregation stood and tearfully waved a white handkerchief in the air to celebrate the faithfulness of God.

JD quickly stepped behind the pulpit and nodded, his signal for the ushers to come forward. At this prearranged sign, the ushers started down the aisle, offering the collection plates in their outstretched hands as the inspired crowd shouted and thanked God for JD's and the children's deliverance from the 18-wheeler.

"What if that had been *you* sitting in that car behind the school bus?"

JD let the question linger a moment, his eyes sweeping the faces of the faithful, making eye contact with as many of them as he could. "Would you be able to say that you were paid up and prayed up? Or do you have unfinished business with God?"

Charlie sensed the guilt and shame of the silent response.

"Today is the day I feel God wants us to catch up on our back tithes and to give a generous offering to our benevolence fund."

JD zeroed in on their undivided attention. "This world is a dangerous place, full of 18-wheelers with faulty maintenance. I wouldn't dare--I wouldn't *dare* think of leaving church this morning without being paid up and right with God. Not one of us knows when we will be called out into eternity to meet the Lord!"

His voice dropped. "If you have any unfinished business with God, *now* is the time to set it right."

He sat down and hung his head as the ushers passed the plates. On cue, the organist began playing "I Surrender All."

Although Charlie had witnessed his dad's dramatic conclusions many times, he found himself pulling out his wallet. He remembered that his neighbor had paid him a hundred dollars for a tune-up he had done on his own time and that he had not yet paid his tithe on that income. Not finding a ten dollar bill in his wallet, he whispered to Nora to grab one from her purse before the collection plate reached them. He wanted the assurance that he and his family were under the mighty hand of God's protection. Paid up and prayed up.

Charlie and Nora had only one child, an eighteen-year-old son, Danny. When Danny walked into a room, he made everyone feel better by simply being there. He was a good kid, and the pride and joy of the entire Davis family.

CHAPTER TWO

Charlie Davis had grown up in Ladner, a small town just north of Springfield in southwestern Missouri. When he was in fourth grade he pedaled papers for *The Springfield Times*, a right-leaning, conservative newspaper that JD, a strong Republican, supported. On occasion, JD had been accused of bullying his congregation into subscribing to the *Times*.

Besides being a dependable paperboy, Charlie showed an aptitude for all things mechanical at an early age. Of all the kids in the neighborhood, he was the only one who knew how to take a bicycle apart, grease the wheel bearings, and put it back together with no leftover parts. As he collected the money from his customers on Saturday mornings, he often gave helpful advice to grown men who were struggling with a stubborn lawnmower they couldn't start. Charlie had an unusual knack for fixing anything with a motor. It was, JD mused, surely a gift.

When Charlie entered high school and went out for football, his coaches recognized that he was something special. He was tough as nails and could run the hundred yard dash in just over ten seconds as a freshman. They expected he would get even faster and were grooming him to be the featured running back on the varsity team. He was destined to become one of the finest high-school athletes Ladner ever produced until he sustained a career-ending knee injury during his sophomore season.

Charlie went on to graduate in the top third of his class but opted to stay in Ladner while many of his classmates went away to college or left Ladner for greener pastures. Charlie worked as a mechanic at the local Chevy dealership and could diagnose an engine problem quicker than any of the other mechanics he worked with. He was a natural when it came to engines, and he quickly won the respect of the guys--even the ones who were old enough to be his father.

CHAPTER THREE

Wednesday morning, three days after the, "paid up and prayed up" sermon, Charlie sleepily reached for the snooze button, half listening for the weather report. The cheerful weatherman reported the high for the day would be 43 degrees with light wind but extreme fog.

As Charlie tapped the button again and drifted off for another few minutes, he heard the distant blast of the horn of a Santa Fe freight train rumbling through town. Only half awake, he thought he heard the far away wail of sirens.

When the radio interrupted his sleep again a few minutes later, he threw back the covers and staggered to the bathroom to start his day. He reached for a fresh shop uniform, ran a comb through his sandy hair, brushed his teeth, and made his way downstairs to the kitchen. As he had hundreds of mornings before, he measured the coffee, poured the water into the coffeemaker, and listened as the pot began to drip with the brew he relied on to start his day. It was a ritual he could do blindfolded. He took his favorite mug from the cabinet and put in some sugar as he waited.

As he reached for the coffee pot, he heard the distant sirens again. Ladner was a town of 1,875, according to the sign posted on the highway near the city limits, and sirens first thing in the morning usually meant trouble. Charlie wondered if there had been an accident caused by the fog. There would probably be lots of fender bender repairs at the dealership over the next day or two.

Still in his slippers and carrying his mug, Charlie walked down the driveway to pick up the newspaper. He couldn't even see his neighbor's house through the thick fog, and he hoped the early morning sun would soon burn it off.

Newspaper in hand, Charlie paused. In the fog, everything seemed so still and quiet at this time of morning. He took a moment to enjoy it and brought the mug to his nose, savoring the smell of his freshly brewed coffee before taking another sip. Back inside, he settled at the kitchen table to enjoy his favorite time of the day--coffee in one hand, the *Times* in the other. Most of the guys at work were avid sports fans, so Charlie reached for the sports page first.

He was startled by a knock at the door. Getting up, he wondered if his neighbor, Bill, was having trouble starting his car again. As he opened the door, he saw two police officers and recognized them immediately. Art Seiffert and Jerry Williams were both known throughout the county. Charlie had worked on their patrol cars several times. In fact, he was the only mechanic they trusted.

Charlie's initial thoughts about "car trouble" faded when he saw the troubled look on Art's face. Art was the one who usually had a joke or something funny to say in every situation. Art was not smiling today as he looked straight at Charlie.

"Charlie, can we come in?"

"Sure, come on in. Anything wrong?"

Art cleared his throat, glanced at Jerry, and spoke softly, "Is Nora still in bed?"

"Sure, she never gets up until 7:30 or so. Why, what's the matter? Why are you here?"

Art looked at the floor. "Charlie, I don't know how to tell you this. We are here to tell you about Danny."

"What about Danny? What do you mean?"

"There's been an accident, Charlie. It involved Danny."

Charlie took a deep breath and shook his head as he processed what he had just heard. *Danny? Accident? Danny's upstairs, asleep.*

He hadn't noticed when he got the paper, but Charlie didn't remember seeing Danny's truck in the driveway. Danny usually parked off to the far side and in the fog Charlie hadn't realized it wasn't there.

"Oh, my God, Art, what happened?" Charlie was panicking. "Where is he? What kind of accident are you talking about?"

It was beginning to fit together. Those awful sirens he had heard earlier.

"Art, where is he? How serious is it? Is he in the hospital?"

Charlie searched Art's face hopefully. Danny always wore his seatbelt, he thought. He can't have been hurt too badly.

"Where is he, what kind of accident was it?" Jerry reached over to take Charlie's arm, trying to maneuver him into a chair. Jerking away, Charlie eyes darted from one man's face to the other.

"Tell me now! What accident? Where's my son?"

Art's voice was barely audible. "Charlie, we have just come from the accident at Devil's Elbow. It's bad, and they are still removing his body from the car."

His body? The words slammed full force into Charlie's mind.

"*His* body? HIS BODY? What are you telling me? I must be dreaming this!" Charlie staggered backward, and both men reached for his arms. An invisible force of fear and panic hit him in the stomach, taking away his breath.

"Where's your wife?"

"She's—she's upstairs in bed." Art and Jerry both looked toward the stairs and then at each other.

"Charlie, you need to get her. We will stay here with you while you tell her."

Jumping to his feet, wild-eyed, Charlie demanded, "No, I have to go to him! I have to find out for myself!"

Charlie bolted out the door, sprinting to his pickup.

"Charlie, don't go out there," Jerry yelled as the storm door slammed behind all three of them. Charlie pulled out his keys and jerked open the truck door, all in one motion. He started his truck and shot off toward Devil's Elbow, tires screaming on the damp pavement. The officers jumped in their squad car in hot pursuit.

Art floored it and flipped on the flashing red lights, afraid of what might happen in the still-thick fog.

Charlie sped through town and past the shop where he had worked for twenty years, fighting for control as he made turns and rounded curves.

He had made this run a thousand times. It was his favorite route when he tested a car he had just tuned up. Passing his dad's church with the neon sign that announced "Jesus Saves!" the truck hit seventy-seven, and Charlie sent up a desperate prayer.

"Oh, Jesus! Please, save my boy! Please, save my boy!"

Even though visibility was only a few yards, Charlie had no fear. Art's words were still thunderous waves pounding in his head, "His body...his body...his body!"

Charlie remembered a story his dad told one Easter about a person who came back to life after being pronounced dead. Maybe Danny had just been knocked out. Maybe his heart stopped for a few minutes and then started again. He had heard about things like that happening. Most everyone in the county knew about that nasty turn at Devil's Elbow. He would get the details later. Right now the only thing that mattered was getting to Danny!

As Charlie got close to Devil's Elbow, he saw the flashing red lights cutting through the fog; then the yellow lights of a tow truck. Flares had been set up to warn other drivers of the accident just ahead. He pulled over into the first area he could and slid to a stop. He threw open the door as the truck stopped, gravel flying. He left the door open and the engine running as he ran full tilt toward the officers.

Devil's Elbow was so named because of the way the road was laid out and for the many accidents that had happened there. Originally, the road had gone straight through to the reservoir, but because the Army Engineers had built a dam and extended the size of the lake, it was necessary to make this turn. Other alternatives were considered, but in the end, all the roads around it were re-engineered. Instead of going straight through, Oak Road veered sharply to the right. Over the years, many drivers had come down the hill and missed the turn. Horror stories were told of cars and trucks alike that had broken through the wooden barricade and gone airborne down the ravine and into the creek that fed into the reservoir. Charlie had pulled many cars out of that ravine when he first worked for the shop. For several years he was the one who made those dreaded late-night wrecker calls.

Art had radioed ahead to warn the State Trooper that Charlie Davis, Danny's father, was on his way.

The fog was still heavy, but the trooper heard Charlie running down the side of the road, his voice hoarse with panic and screaming, "Where is he? Where's my boy?"

"Mr. Davis, don't go down there!"

Paying no attention, Charlie, a man possessed, slid and stumbled down the steep creek bank. A special tow truck, with hydraulic jaws designed to pull apart the heavy metal had been summoned from Springfield to aid in removing the victim.

Scrambling down the embankment toward Danny's truck, his heart pounding, Charlie surveyed the scene. Danny's pickup, instead of turning, had gone straight over the embankment and down toward the creek below. The front of the blue truck was nose down in two feet of water. The cab was not under water but was crunched by the force of the impact. Sliding down the muddy creek bank, Charlie lost both slippers thrashing his way through the water toward the truck.

"Charlie, don't go over there! Don't do it! You don't want to see this!" Charlie didn't hear the officers pleading with him. He had only one thing in mind and that was to find and rescue his boy.

The police report would later show that Danny's pickup had flown through the air for about sixty feet before landing nose down. The truck hit the creek bed with such force that it jammed the steering column back up and into Danny's chest. From the spider-like cracks in the windshield, it was obvious his head had hit with tremendous force. The official police report would reveal that he died instantly.

The accident was phoned in by the Snapp brothers who lived nearby and had just come in from a night of fishing off the bridge at the reservoir. The first officers to arrive scrambled down to the truck and, finding no pulse, knew the driver was dead. After running a quick check from the license plate, the authorities knew it was Danny Davis. Soon after, Art and Jerry were called to make the notification of death.

While the officers waited for the tow truck to arrive from Springfield, one of them went to his squad car and pulled a gray blanket from the trunk. Another officer helped spread the blanket over Danny's head and upper body. It appeared he had been dead for several minutes, maybe as much as an hour or two, before they had been notified of the accident.

When Charlie arrived, there were four squad cars managing the accident scene. Prior to his arrival, they were struggling to get the broken steering column away from Danny's chest. They were having a difficult time of it. One of the workers, one who didn't know Charlie, suggested the best thing was to hook up the cable from the wrecker to the back of the pickup. Then, they could use the wench to pull it out of the ravine with Danny's body still in it, load it up, and take the truck on back to the shop where they had a cutting torch and could cut away the metal. The ranking officer knew Charlie and vetoed that idea. He knew Charlie would never allow his son's body to be taken away in such a manner.

The panicked dad grabbed the tailgate, breathless and white-faced as he sloshed around to the driver's side. The back of the truck had looked normal, but he could now see that it was worse than he thought, worse than any accident he had ever seen in this ravine. One of the officers standing by the driver's door of the truck with a flashlight in his hand, ordered Charlie to stay back, but it was useless to try to stop him. Charlie approached the officer and screamed, "That's my son in there! Get the hell out of my way!"

"Oh, God! Oh, God! Oh, God!" Charlie screamed as he saw the cracks in the windshield just above the dash. He knew from experience that something had hit it with a tremendous force. He stepped closer and saw the bent steering column had been forced up and into the driver hidden under the blanket. Charlie, terrified of what he might find under the gray covering half prayed as he gently lifted the edge of the blanket. "Oh, God! Oh, Jesus.

Please, don't let this be Danny!"

Knowing the young person inside the truck was dead, there was a sense of resignation among the officers, not the usual frenzy when seconds matter and someone inside is fighting for their life. A few moments earlier, when they saw Charlie running wildly through the water toward the truck, they froze, knowing they were about to witness a moment no person ever wants to see; that unspeakable moment when a father realizes the light of his heart has been blown out forever. All activity among the officers stopped as Charlie reached for the edge of the gray blanket.

"Don't do this Charlie, you *don't* want to see this!" Ignoring his pleas, Charlie continued, took hold of the corner of the blanket and gently pulled it back.

When Danny was a newborn, Charlie took an active role in helping Nora with his care. He couldn't count the times he quietly slipped into the nursery and gently lifted the blanket over his son. As a baby, Danny often kicked the cover off while sleeping, but Charlie didn't mind slipping the soft blanket back up to his neck to keep him warm.

This time, Charlie pulled back a blanket to uncover the face of his teen-age son. Danny was dead.

CHAPTER FOUR

Danny Davis had grown up in Ladner, just like his dad. He also had a paper route when he was eleven, and nearly everyone knew him as JD's grandson. He had good parents, upstanding grandparents, and everyone in town liked him. He had grown to six feet tall, 150 pounds, and he was very athletic. He had brown hair, hazel eyes and a smile that lit up the room when he walked in. He followed in his dad's footsteps as one of the outstanding athletes, not only of Ladner but the entire county. He played football and baseball for the high school and lettered in both sports during his sophomore, junior, and senior years. Academically, he was in the top ten percent of his class and was loved by his fellow students.

Initially, it was thought the fatal wounds to Danny's body had been caused by two things: the impact of his head hitting the windshield that caused his neck to break and the force of the steering column slamming into his chest.

When Charlie saw Danny's face, he wanted to turn away and pretend it hadn't happened. But at the same time, he could not take his eyes off the beautiful face of his son. The boy's eyes were closed and a blood-soaked lock of hair drooped down the side of his forehead. There was a trail of blood coming from the corner of his mouth.

When Charlie saw Danny's face, screams erupted from his throat as he shook Danny's shoulder, "Danny, Danny, please, say something! Danny, Danny, can you hear me?" Charlie's eyes were wild as he continued to scream. "It's me, Dad! Oh, God, Danny! Danny, please, please! Danny, Danny! It's okay. I'm going to get you out of here! Danny!"

Even as he screamed for Danny to respond, Charlie shook his son's shoulder, praying he would open his eyes and start breathing. But deep down, Charlie knew nothing would ever be the same.

Charlie dropped the edge of the blanket and sloshed backwards in the water. The two officers nearby grabbed his arms and held him, trying to ease him back to the creek bank where he could sit down. All of a sudden, Charlie's knees were weak. The horrible realization that Danny was gone exploded in his mind. It was as though lightning had hit his brain, shattering it into a million pieces.

The officers guided him to a spot not far from the truck. He sat on a large rock, numb, both legs still in the icy water. He was going into shock and felt nothing. As soon as he dropped down on the rock, his hands covered his face.

"Oh, God, this isn't supposed to happen to me." His dad's sermon about being paid up and prayed up seemed like a joke as he wrapped both arms around himself and screamed out his sorrow. The two who had walked him away from the truck looked away. Charlie's wailing and brokenness were too much even for seasoned officers to bear.

Up on the road, police officers who knew Charlie, were also in reverent silence. The accident scene was ablaze with lights from their squad cars, and for a moment it seemed as though they were witnessing a tragedy on an outdoor stage. They had watched

Charley's dogged persistence in getting to the wrecked pickup. Then, when Charlie knew for sure his son was gone, they heard his awful screams echoing through the woods. One officer walked away a few yards to stand by his patrol car, head down, bracing himself with one hand on the top of his car.

Charlie, his feet still in the cold stream, continued rocking back and forth, deep moans coming from his throat.

The officers nearby wanted to help him, but his pain was beyond consolation. Nothing they could do or say would bring the boy in the truck back to life.

The officers gave Charlie some time alone, nodded to each other, then reached down, took his arms and lifted him to his feet. They knew Charlie was in shock, the previous fight and resistance drained from him. Now, there was only sad resignation as he allowed them to lead him through the mud and weeds. Other officers helped by using the glow from their large flashlights to illuminate the make-shift path to help them find their way up to the road.

One officer asked Charlie for the keys to his truck, and Charlie mumbled they were still in the truck, which the officer discovered, driver's-side door still open.

When Charlie's knees buckled, the men eased him down along the side of the road to wait for his truck to arrive. He was in shock, and it was as if he had resigned himself to do whatever they asked him to do.

Art and Jerry had not followed Charlie down the creek bank to the wreckage but had remained on the road above, hearing the unforgettable screams.

"We're going to take you home now, Charlie. We'll take good care of you." Art walked Charlie to the passenger door, helped him in, reached across and pulled the seatbelt across Charlie's body, and clicked it in place. Jerry got into the squad car to follow them back to the Davis home.

The rescue team watched them leave. No one moved or spoke until the lights on Charlie's truck disappeared.

The sun had not yet broken through the fog that was as thick as the awful silence inside the truck where Charlie sat motionless, staring into the darkness. Art was dreading the task ahead of telling Nora.

CHAPTER FIVE

Charlie broke a cold sweat as he contemplated forcing himself to speak the awful words. He silently prayed for strength to deliver the shattering message.

As they turned into the driveway, Art turned to Charlie, "Do you want me to tell her?"

"No, I'll do it."

Art was out of the truck first, and he walked around to the passenger side and took Charlie's arm as they moved toward the front door. He heard the squad car's door close and knew Jerry was coming right behind them. The brass knob on the front door was cool in Charlie's hand as he slowly pushed it open.

Nora was in the kitchen. She looked up, puzzled, when the door opened and the men stepped inside. She put her cup on the nearby counter.

"What on earth is going on, Charlie?" She had heard the commotion when Charlie left earlier, and she, too, had heard the sirens, but had gone back to sleep. When she got up later and Charlie was gone she had begun to feel concerned. She was accustomed to him sometimes leaving early to help someone with a car emergency, but it was highly unusual for him to leave without a word or leaving a note

Charlie was barefoot, his feet muddy. The legs of his blue shop pants were wet, his features pale and drawn. He seemed unable to speak.

"Nora." He looked at the floor, then tried again. "Nora, Danny has been in an accident, and..." She froze and searched his face. "No, no! Don't say it."

"Nora, Danny didn't make it!"

She reached out for the kitchen counter. "Charlie, Danny is upstairs in bed!"

Charlie couldn't speak. He slowly shook his head.

Nora ran toward Danny's room, taking the stairs two at a time. Throwing the door open, she turned on the light to find his empty, perfectly made-up bed.

Charlie was right behind her. She spun around and grabbed his shoulders.

"Where is he? What happened?"

"There was an accident on Devil's Elbow. I don't know what happened. His truck went off the road and down into the creek." Nora tried to process his words.

"Why was he out there? How... how?"

Charlie instinctively wrapped his arms around his terrified wife. There was nothing to do but hold her as she screamed her anguished protests into his shoulder. As the merciful tranquilizer of shock overtook her, Charlie led her back down the stairs into the hellish nightmare that would become their new normal.

With Art's help, Charlie got Nora to the couch. "Danny, Danny, no, Danny." She covered her chest with her hands as though her heart would surely burst.

Art watched helplessly as Charlie and Nora moaned as if they were in physical pain. Art had witnessed similar tragedies a few times during his career, and each time he tried to imagine how he would survive losing one of his own children.

Several years earlier, he was the officer who notified Bonnie Craig, another mother in Ladner, about the death of her husband and son who were returning home from a ballgame. Both of her sons were in the car, one sitting in the front with him, the other in the back seat. A drunk driver, traveling the opposite direction at 105 mph, veered into the median. His car went airborne, crashing down into the Craig car, instantly killing the father and the son in the front seat.

Art recalled his helplessness when he told Bonnie that her husband and son had died. That mother, like Nora, went into shock when she heard the news that her husband and youngest son were dead. The younger boy always rode in the front seat and the older boy always rode in back. Art would never forget driving Bonnie Craig to the hospital where the surviving son was in surgery, fighting for his life. In the Emergency Room, the nurses gave Bonnie the boy's bloody clothes. Suddenly, she screamed as she realized from the clothes just handed to her that she had been wrong. The son she thought was dead was alive, and the son she thought was alive was dead. It was one of grief's cruelest moments, one he would never forget.

Art sat with the grieving wife and mother waiting for the outcome of the surviving son's surgery. As they waited, she became calm as she turned to Art.

"Can you answer a question for me?"

"I'll try."

"Today, I lost my husband and my son. Can you tell me why I am crying more for my son than for my husband?"

Art remembered mumbling something about a mother's instinct to protect her child, but felt unqualified to answer her probing question. From his experience that night, he had concluded that losing a young child was more traumatic for a woman than losing her husband.

Art took a seat close to Charlie and Nora, helpless to ease their pain. He knew how to write a ticket, how to arrest a drunk, how to investigate a robbery or a burglary, but in cases like this, he was clueless. After what seemed like a long time, Charlie and Nora turned to Art.

"What should we do now?" Nora asked.

Art pushed a box of tissues toward her. "Who can I call for you?" Art knew they needed someone with them as soon as possible, and it was at this point he usually asked if he could call a family member or a pastor. In this case, that next of kin and pastor were the same: The Reverend JD.

⇒⊹⇐

A call before 8:00 a.m. most always brought bad news. "This is the parsonage, Pastor JD speaking."

"Daddy, can you come over right now?"

"Charlie, what's wrong?"

"Daddy, please. Just come now. Danny has been in an accident."

"Charlie, what happened, is he okay? What kind of accident? Is he hurt? I'll call the prayer line and ask everyone to start praying."

"Just come, Dad, please. Just come now." Charlie ended the call.

JD hurried down the hall to the bedroom where Anna was getting dressed.

"We need to go, Anna. Now." Sensing the urgency, she reacted quickly and they were out the door in a matter of minutes.

As they neared Charlie's house, they saw the police car. Anna's hands were tightly clenched as JD wheeled into the driveway.

JD got to the porch first and dread gripped his heart when a police officer opened the door. Art motioned them in. When Charlie saw his dad, he nearly collapsed into his arms.

"Oh, Daddy! He's gone, Danny's gone."

"Son, what happened?" JD tried to interrogate his sobbing son.

"Daddy, he's gone – an accident at Devil's Elbow."

Anna moved to the couch and wrapped both arms around Nora. She, too, began to moan as the unimaginable settled in.

The light of their lives had been extinguished. No one said it, but they all wondered, *Where is God?*

CHAPTER SIX

J D had comforted hundreds of grieving parishioners across the years. He knew just what to say and just how to instruct them on what needed to be done. But this was different. This wasn't just a family in the church; this was *his* family.

Oh, Jesus, help me now, he prayed silently.

As JD turned to Art and began asking questions, Art tried to answer without disclosing too many details; those could come later. But JD heard enough to accept that his grandson was dead. Steeling himself to his own feelings, he walked into the kitchen and called Stella Watkins, one of the faithful members of his congregation and the person in charge of coordinating the church's bereavement ministry. Stella would contact those who would see to it that the family's immediate need for sustenance was met.

JD returned to the living room and approached Charlie. "Son, tell me what you know. Was there another car involved? Did he fall asleep? When did it happen?" The questions were like rapid shots from a machine gun, demanding Charlie's response.

"I don't know, Dad. They came and told me around six this morning. I just know that he's gone--gone! Oh, God, this can't be happening."

His own heart breaking, JD looked squarely into his son's eyes and reverted back to his standard pastoral responses. "Charlie, we must not question the ways of God. There is a reason for this, son, and we need to hang on and trust in the wise ways of our Heavenly Father."

Charlie barely heard the feeble explanation.

CHAPTER SEVEN

Mick Thompson, or Mickey, as most people called him, owned the only mortuary in Ladner. He was a short man just over five feet tall and slight of build. At 58, he had a weakness for cigars imported from Havana. He wore his gray hair short and neatly combed and was always dressed in black dress pants and a long-sleeved white shirt with a black band around his upper arm. His father and grandfather before him had worn a black band, so Mickey felt bound by the tradition and was never seen without it. Mickey's smile was friendly and open, his demeanor was reassuring.

Mickey had inherited Thompson Mortuary from his father, who had inherited it from his father. Mickey loved to tell stories of riding in funeral processions next to his grandfather on the seat of the stately carriage that was pulled by a team of black Arabians. Mickey told of holding the reins of the six-horse team as it marched proudly through town. He recalled that it was common in those days for the townspeople to stand in silence by the road, men with hats in their hands, as an important city official was taken to his final resting place. He had told the story of the mayor's funeral to just about everyone in Ladner.

When it came to working with the ministers in Ladner, Mickey had his favorites. John Davis was not one of them. So, on that morning, when Mickey was told the ambulance was on its way with the body of Danny Davis, he felt uneasy. He knew this was going to be a big funeral that would, no doubt, be held in JD's church. Mickey prepared himself mentally, knowing that JD liked to take control of every funeral, and this funeral was going to be a very special one.

After Danny's body was removed from the scene of the accident, the tow truck's long cable was attached to Danny's wrecked pickup. Soon, the engine of the wrecker revved as the cable tightened. The demolished truck reluctantly moved backwards up the muddy creek bank. As it came out of the ravine, the officers in charge of the accident scene began to examine the truck again; this time more closely. They looked inside the cab for signs of alcohol, but there was no indication the accident was alcohol related. *The guardrail was so clearly marked. What could have caused Danny to drive straight through it without even trying to stop?*

Danny Davis had been known to push the speed limit from time to time. Still, it appeared he had driven straight through the barrier, which was marked with red reflectors, and into the ravine. When the mangled mass of metal was pulled to the road, the tow truck slowly pulled away from the scene. In the morning light, the officers searched for skid marks. There were none.

CHAPTER EIGHT

Danny was pronounced dead at the scene by the coroner, and JD rightly assumed that his body would be taken to Thompson Mortuary. He knew the bereavement team would be coming to Charlie and Nora's with cinnamon rolls, fruit, and coffee any time now, and it would be the first of many meals the team would deliver to the front door in the coming days.

JD began making a mental list of who should be called, and he thought immediately of Danny's girlfriend. He asked if anyone had called Sandy. Charlie and Nora looked at each other; neither had thought about her.

Nora turned to Charlie. "We should tell her before she hears it from someone else."

JD spoke up as though it was his decision as he reached for the phone, "I can call and talk to her parents right now."

"No, Dad," Charlie said. "I think we should go over there and tell her in person."

Sandy Peterson was 17 years old with shiny, shoulder-length black hair, dark eyes, and dimples. She was athletic, the captain of the high school cheerleading squad, and an honor student. She also worked part time as a waitress at the Boar's Head, one of the favorite restaurants in town. She and Danny had been dating exclusively, and they both believed that they would marry someday. She daydreamed that they start their family in Ladner, reasoning that she could work and support them while Danny finished college.

Sandy was showered and dressed and about to have breakfast when she heard the knock at the front door. Her mother was upstairs and her dad had left for work, so she went to open the door. She was surprised to see Danny's dad and grandfather, but she invited them in. She could tell by their faces that something was wrong.

Charlie, his voice barely audible, spoke first. "Sandy, is your mom at home?"

"Sure, she's upstairs." Searching their faces, she called for her mother. "Mom, can you come down? We have company."

As Gloria descended the stairs, she looked expectantly at Charlie and JD. "Well, this is a surprise. What can I do for you this morning?"

"Sandy, I have some bad news about Danny." Charlie hesitated.

Sandy took a step back, the color draining from her face. "What's wrong with him?

Charlie and Nora had also hoped, although without mentioning it, that Sandy and Danny would end up together. They thought Sandy was a lovely, level-headed girl who would be a welcome addition to their small family.

Charlie looked straight into her eyes. "Sandy, Danny was in an accident out at Devil's Elbow last night." Charlie felt like the words were strangling him, but he went on. "We don't know for sure what caused it, but, Sandy—he--he didn't make it. Danny's dead."

Sandy staggered backwards, her hands to her mouth. She searched their faces. "That isn't true!"

Gloria wrapped her arms tightly around Sandy in a vain effort to absorb some of the pain from her daughter.

Gloria held her daughter and rocked her in her arms as Charlie and JD stood in silence as she wept for him.

Instantly, Sandy tore herself away from her mother's arms and ran upstairs and into the bathroom. Gloria, Charlie, and JD, could hear her vomiting as she called Danny's name over and over. As Gloria hurried up the stairs to her daughter, JD told her that they would be in touch.

They let themselves out but could still hear Sandy's cries through the closed door.

CHAPTER NINE

P hones across town were ringing as the awful news spread.
"Did Danny really die in an accident?"
"What happened?"
"Was he run off the road?"

When the Davis phone began ringing, Anna answered.
She knew no details, only that Danny had, indeed, lost his life.
Answering the calls somehow gave her a break from her own overwhelming grief, and it felt almost as though she was talking about
some other family and someone else's beloved grandson. Not her
precious Danny.

Pushing his own personal devastation aside, JD went about the
task of helping Charlie and Nora steel themselves against their
emotions and deal with the task of making funeral arrangements.
Under ordinary circumstances, he would go into the home of the
bereaved and help plan the funeral while someone else assumed
the role of holding the family together. But now, he took on both
roles, determined to be strong and think clearly while trying not
to think about his own crushing loss.

When Stella's team arrived with food and drink for the family, JD tried his best to get Charlie, Nora and Anna to the small kitchen table to eat something. He knew they would need nourishment for that day and the days to come. It was not an easy undertaking. It was like chewing cardboard, and swallowing was a task that seemed unfamiliar and too hard to accomplish. Eating didn't matter to them; nothing mattered.

JD reached in his pocket for the small New Testament that was always with him, knowing he needed to get his loved ones focused on the Word of God and the promise of seeing Danny again in heaven. He quickly found the fourteenth chapter of the Gospel of John. It was the King James Version of the Bible, the only translation that God had truly blessed, as far as JD was concerned. He was so adamant about the KJV that it was announced on the sign in front of the church--Ladner Full Gospel Fellowship Church: *King James Bible.* JD wanted everyone to know that while every other church in town had gone to The Living Bible or some other watered-down version, *his* church was going to stick with the version that had brought blessing to the world through all generations. To JD, the King James was the only true Bible. Folks needed to know that before they walked through the double doors of his church.

He began to read, "Let not your heart be troubled, if ye believe in God, believe also in me. I go to prepare a place for you and if I go, I will come again and receive you unto myself so that where I am, ye may be also."

After reading, JD cleared his throat. "Let's pray."

He led the family in a short prayer, asking God to give them comfort as they faced this nightmare. He thanked God that Danny was now with Jesus and closed the prayer by asking God to help them as they planned the funeral.

He then took out a small pad of paper and pen from his suit pocket and started a to-do list. He already knew that Mickey Thompson would prepare Danny's body; nothing could be done about that. Everyone in Ladner expected Thompson to handle the funeral.

"I suppose they have taken his body to Thompson's place."

Charlie and Nora both nodded.

"And, I suppose he will be calling you soon and will want you to come make arrangements for the funeral. I'll be there to guide you through this whole process. I've done it hundreds of times."

JD leaned back in the kitchen chair, raising his voice as he assumed more authority. "However, before we see Mickey, we must get the jump on this and try to make some decisions ourselves."

Feeling in control now, JD continued. "I know Mickey's won't be nearly large enough to handle the crowd that will attend the visitation and funeral. We'll need to have both of those at the church." Nora nodded, but Charlie's mind was still back at the scene of the accident.

While JD talked funeral details, Charlie mind was fixated on the accident scene: Danny's body, his neck broken, the small stream of blood coming from his mouth; it was permanently seared into his brain. Uppermost in his mind the question loomed: *Why? Why did this happen? Why did Danny drive straight through that barricade? Did the brakes fail? Was he distracted? Did he miss the turn because of the fog?* These questions and others looped again and again through his mind. *Why has this happened to me and my family? Is this payback for my past sins and mistakes? Why did God do this to me--to us?*

As JD talked on about the music, the casket, the casket bearers, the flowers, Charlie looked up and interrupted. "Daddy, we are sitting here talking about Danny's funeral, and I can't believe it's happening. Yesterday at this time he was right here, sitting at this table."

Charlie buried his face in his hands, his voice breaking. "And here we are, planning his funeral. Why did God let this happen? We've always tried to do the right thing, haven't we? God is supposed to protect us—take care of us. Didn't you just say last Sunday that things like this don't happen to people who are prayed up and paid up?" Charlie searched JD's face for an answer. "Daddy, can you tell me why?"

JD was clearly shaken. "Yes, son, I know it's hard, but we must not question the wisdom of God. We must simply go on and trust in his sovereign will."

As JD side-stepped Charlie's question and tried to keep his family focused on planning Danny's funeral, the news of Danny's death was spreading throughout Ladner.

Phones began to ring and people walked or drove to the shop where the truck had been taken—the very shop where Charlie worked. They wanted to see it for themselves. Everyone in town knew who drove that truck.

CHAPTER TEN

Mickey Thompson called the Davis home around 11:00 o'clock, expressing his sympathy and assuring Charlie that he would do everything in his power to make the funeral a fitting tribute to Danny. They agreed that Charlie and Nora would meet Mickey at his office that afternoon, and Mickey asked them to bring along the clothes they wanted Danny to be buried in.

The fog was gone and shafts of light from the morning sun were streaming through the window when Nora pushed open the door to Danny's room. It was cluttered with the mementos of his life, everything in the exact place it had been the last time Danny awoke in his bedroom. *Could it really have been just yesterday morning?* Sports trophies, T-shirts, the quilt his grandmother had made for him by hand, his backpack, a half-used meal ticket for his school lunches, ticket stubs from a concert he and Sandy had attended, the pillow where his head should be resting. She closed her eyes and pictured him there, stretching and yawning, hungry for breakfast.

She crossed the room to his closet where more T-shirts, blue jeans, button-up shirts hung. In the back were the sport coat and suit he seldom wore. On a hook on the back of the door hung a bathrobe. She took it from the hook and held it in both hands, burying her face in the scent of her son. Nora could feel him, hear him, smell him, his arms pulling her into a hug, "I love you, Mom. You're the best!" Danny thought she was beautiful, and he was always so proud of her, always happy to be with her, never getting too big to take her hand or show his affection for her or try to avoid her in front of his friends the way many of his friends did with their moms.

She decided on the sport coat. It was off-white, and the light blue shirt would go well with it. There was no guessing about his tie. He would wear his favorite; black with white polka dots. Danny had complimented his uncle on it one night when they were all out to dinner. A few days later, the gift-wrapped tie arrived in the mail with a sweet note from his uncle. Danny treasured that silly tie and wore it proudly. She knew this was the only tie that would fit this occasion.

She quickly pulled out a pair of black slacks and a belt and put everything in an overnight duffle bag she retrieved from under the bed. Her grief was so heavy as she walked down the stairs that she felt she might collapse under its weight.

CHAPTER ELEVEN

Nora called and asked Sandy if she would like to join them when they went to Thompson Funeral Home to meet with Mickey. JD and Anna were coming too.

Thompson Funeral Home was located on a mainly residential street in an old and plain two-story red-brick building. It looked just like all the other houses on the block except for a small sign on the front porch and the small asphalt parking lot behind it.

Charlie had never paid much attention to the funeral home before. Today, he felt his pulse quicken as his hand touched the cold brass doorknob and pushed the door open. As he held it for the others, he thought he would never pass this place again without remembering today.

Opening the door triggered a soft chime-like bell that rang in Mickey's office. Mickey quickly snuffed out his cigar and made his way to greet them, waving his hands to clear the cigar smoke from the air. By the time he held out his welcoming hand, he was wearing his sad and solemn, yet comforting, smile. He spoke softly as he led them to his office where he offered water and coffee. They all declined except for Sandy, who accepted a small cup of water. The stale cigar smoke had unsettled her still-queasy stomach.

Mickey leaned back in his leather chair, and looked at Charlie. "I never dreamed we would be faced with making these arrangements for Danny. Has anyone figured out yet what happened?"

"No, we are still trying to figure that out. We don't know why he was out there at that time of night. No one has found anything wrong with the truck." Charlie looked at the floor. "We only know he didn't make the turn at Devil's Elbow and..." His voice trailed off as silent tears rolled down his face.

Nora was holding Sandy's hand in hers. Sandy seemed about to speak, but swallowed her words. Her eyes filled with tears and she stared unseeingly at the front of Mickey's desk.

Mickey knew too much discussion about the accident or Danny's injuries would add to the family's anguish, so he began asking questions about Danny and what the family wanted to include in his obituary. They had missed the official cut-off to make tomorrow's paper, but he hoped that if they hurried he might pull some strings and convince the copyeditor to squeeze it in.

Mickey led them through the standard information needed to put together the death notice: Date of birth, date of death, survivors, preceded in death by....

Charlie suggested to Nora that they include Sandy in the survivors. "Danny told me he intended to marry her someday." Nora nodded.

JD cleared his throat, looked at Sandy and spoke for the first time. "We should think twice about this. I don't think you will want to be listed as Danny's fiancée. Although you might not think so now, someday you will likely find another young man and might look back on this written record with regret." It was agreed that Sandy would be listed as Danny's sweetheart.

The remainder listed Danny's accomplishments as the captain of the baseball team, a member of the all-county football team as starting running back, his love of fishing. The time and place for the visitation and funeral service were decided upon.

As JD and Anna and Nora made decisions on the details, Charlie began to think about his own obituary and how it would look: preceded in death by his only son, Danny. No grandchildren. The crushing death of his son also meant the death of hopes and dreams. His future, as well as his present, had died with Danny.

Charlie's attention was drawn back to the business at hand by JD's no-nonsense voice. "Mickey, we have already decided that both the visitation and the funeral service will be held in my church."

Mickey hated transporting bodies to other locations, but there was no sense in engaging in a battle he couldn't win. He leaned back in his chair with a sigh of resignation. "Of course. When do you want to schedule the visitation and service?"

JD looked at Charlie and Nora. Neither one of them seemed able to make that decision. Charlie shrugged slightly and met JD's eyes. It was all the encouragement JD needed to move forward with the decision.

"If the obituary is in tomorrow's paper, I think we can have the visitation on Friday night and the funeral on Saturday at 10:00 a.m. We can hold the funeral dinner in the Fellowship Hall following the funeral and the graveside service."

Mickey was taking notes and agreed that he and his staff could accommodate them. Aside from choosing the casket and vault, the only thing left to discuss was Danny's final resting place. There was just one cemetery in Ladner and it was the same place where many of Nora's and Charlie's relatives were buried. So, the obituary would read that Danny would be buried in the Oak Grove Cemetery.

Mickey moved from his desk and asked Danny's parents and grandparents and Sandy to follow him. "I am going to show you the caskets we have in the next room. You will find a wide range of colors and quality. Some of them are made of expensive hard woods that have been imported and others are simply plywood covered with inexpensive fabric. I'll wait outside the room, because I know this is a very important decision that you will make only once, and I don't want to interfere. The prices are printed on a small card sitting on each casket."

Nora and Sandy held hands as they slowly moved along the row of caskets. Nora knew the final decision would be up to her and Sandy. There were twelve caskets. Nora ignored the prices and began to think about the outfit she had already chosen and how it would look against the fabric inside. She knew the color had to be some shade of blue. She found one that suited her and turned to Sandy. "What do you think of this one?"

Sandy reached out and touched the cold, shiny metal and nodded. "I think its fine."

CHAPTER TWELVE

Danny and his friends in the youth group had gotten in trouble once for throwing rocks at Claude Ellis's tombstone from the steps of JD's church. No one liked Claude anyway, and the boys had heard JD use Claude's life as an illustration a couple times. The proximity of the cemetery came in handy when JD preached on the finality of death and eternity, which was often.

One of his favorite sermon texts was found in James. "For what is your life? It is just a vapor that appeareth for a little time, and then vanisheth away." His voice reverberated through the sanctuary as he often walked to the front of the altar and pointed through the large side windows that faced the cemetery. The monuments in the cemetery were easy to see, and it irritated JD if folks didn't turn to look through the window as he pointed in that direction.

"Look out there! Look out there, because we will all end up there someday!" JD used such drama to scare people into coming forward and confessing their sins at the altar.

When Charlie and Nora drove through gates of the cemetery to choose Danny's burial plot, they noticed the dark blue sedan of the cemetery salesman, who identified himself as the representative of the nearby monument and cemetery management firm. He asked them to follow him to an area he thought they might find suitable for Danny's final resting place. After a short drive the salesman pulled over and Charlie pulled in behind him. Both he and Nora got out of the car and walked the short distance to the site.

It was a cool day for spring, and the wind made it seem even cooler. After looking at their choices, they chose three plots under an oak tree and close to the road; one for Danny and two for themselves to be used when the time came. As the salesman retreated to his car to write up the paperwork, Charlie and Nora stood in the cold, windswept cemetery, in shock and hoping they were in a bad dream.

The contract the salesman produced stipulated three 600-dollar funeral plots to be paid over time, plus interest. Charlie and Nora signed the document without reading it. As the salesman handed the signed contract over to Charlie, he mumbled his sympathy for the death of their son. Charlie felt as if he had already heard "I'm so sorry" a thousand times.

Mary, the Davis's next-door neighbor had answered the phone at their house while Charlie and Nora were at the cemetery. She had fielded numerous calls asking if the news they had received of Danny's death was accurate; others called offering their condolences. Mary had also received food from Stella's team and other friends

There were a few cars parked on the street in front of Charlie's and Nora's house and in front of their neighbors' houses as Charlie pulled into the driveway and stared at the front door before turning to Nora. "It looks like we have company. We might as well go in and face them and get it over with. There's no way to escape it."

Inside, they were greeted by the once-welcomed sweet aroma of cinnamon rolls and coffee. Today, the smell of it made Charlie feel a little sick.

CHAPTER THIRTEEN

When Danny's wrecked and muddy pickup truck was towed into town and parked at the garage where Charlie worked, it wasn't long until people gathered around to inspect it. When Charlie's fellow mechanics arrived for work and saw the truck parked by the body shop, they were horrified to hear that it belonged to Danny and that he had not survived the accident.

Pat Brown, who worked in the stall next to Charlie, had two boys, Kyle and Stanley, who were good friends with both Danny and Sandy. Pat's specialty was transmissions, but when he heard the wrecked truck outside was Danny's, he hurried out to inspect it.

He gathered with the others around the truck, trying to understand what had happened. They all walked around staring at the mangled metal. No one spoke as each wondered what might have caused the accident. Danny wasn't a drug or alcohol user and wasn't known to run with troublemakers. Most of the guys in the shop could take one look at a wreck and quickly figure out what happened, especially if they knew who owned it. But no one had a clue as they looked at Danny's pickup. As Pat and the others walked back into the shop with heavy hearts, each one of them worried for Charlie; he loved Danny more than his own life.

Buck's Sales and Service was named for its owner, Buck McCoy. He was a little guy who had recognized, as a young man, that there was a strong need for a reliable and trusted repair shop in Ladner. He hired expert mechanics as well as young men who showed mechanical aptitude. Charlie Davis was his top mechanic. When the news of Danny's death hit the shop, everyone knew the effect it would have on the Davis family as well as the shop family. A dark cloud hung over the entire work force.

When Buck drove up to his shop and walked inside, he was given the news. Unbuttoning his coat, he walked into the office, and Angie, one of the two office girls, tearfully greeted him. As was the custom at the shop, there was a jar on her desk with a small, handwritten note next to it explaining the jar was there for shop employees to contribute for flowers. There was also a place for employees to sign up to help provide meals for the Davis family. Everyone at the shop knew that Charlie and Nora would need support for many days to come.

Danny was eight years old when he started coming to the shop with Charlie on Saturday mornings, when the shop was open only until noon. Charlie showed Danny how to clean engine parts and how to use a shop rag to wipe the dirt and oil from the tools. Sometimes Danny held the shop light just right for Charlie so he could see better into hard-to-reach places on an engine, or he would ask Danny to fetch a certain tool from the toolbox. Danny also offered help to the other mechanics when he was there. Everyone at Buck's liked Danny.

Across the street from Buck's garage was the Boar's Head, the restaurant and diner where Charlie met up with Tom, Tiny, and Al nearly every morning. Charlie was the only one of the four who still worked full time.

Tom was a 68-year-old widower who was semi-retired. He was a skilled handyman who took on occasional odd jobs that most others wouldn't touch.

Tiny Turner always walked to the Boar's Head from his home. He was called Tiny, but he was far from small. It was an eight-minute walk exactly, and he always arrived at 7 a.m. on the dot.

Al wore a ball cap that he removed as he walked through the door. He was former military, and he kept in shape by riding a bike to the Boar's Head every morning. He wore a backpack in which he carried a newspaper, a dictionary, and a bottle of water. If he became bored or the conversation lagged, he pulled out the newspaper and went to work on the crossword puzzle. Besides the well-worn dictionary, he always had a book inside the backpack that he could pull out and read.

The Boar's Head had just one waitress who worked the breakfast shift. Maria was a thirty-one year old single parent who lived with her mother which was within walking distance of the cafe. She was quick on her feet and had a great memory for taking food orders. She never wrote anything down and rarely made a mistake.

As the three men gathered to eat, Al looked at his pocket watch, "Charlie's late today."

Maria came to their table. "Did you hear what happened to Danny Davis last night?"

Al reached for the sugar. "Nope, what happened?"

Maria, knew how close the three men were to Charlie, so she quietly shared the news of Danny's accident and death.

They sat in stunned silence. These three knew, more than most, just how much Charlie loved his son. As they contemplated the magnitude of what they had heard, they were at a loss for words, just staring into their coffee mugs.

Finally, Tom looked up at Maria and asked the obvious question. "Does anyone know how it happened?"

Maria shook her head. "I just know that his truck went straight through the barricade into the air and landed nose-down in the creek."

Tom let out a low whistle. "Man, I know that area very well. I've parked close to that exact place and walked down that ravine to my favorite fishing hole. It's a steep drop from the road.

Silence fell again as they pondered the same questions. *How did this happen? Danny seemed like a responsible kid. Did he take his own life? Was he drinking or using drugs? Did the brakes go out? It didn't make any sense that Danny Davis, a healthy, popular, fun-loving kid would drive to certain death right through the barricade that was so clearly marked.*

After a few minutes they began to talk about ways they might be able to help Charlie. Maria found a clean, one-quart Mason jar, scribbled a note, taped it to the jar, and set it beside the cash register. The Davis family was known to just about everyone in Ladner, and she knew the customers of the Boar's Head would want to give toward flowers for Danny's funeral.

She figured the funeral would be one of the biggest Ladner had seen in a long time.

CHAPTER FOURTEEN

J D, unable to sleep, arrived at his church office while it was still dark. Flipping on the light, he slumped into the leather chair behind his desk. Reaching for his Bible, he bowed his head. *Lord, if ever I've needed help preparing for a funeral, I need it now. No funeral I've taken part in has prepared me for this. Guide me, God, and give me the strength I need to do it.*

Taking out a pen, he reached for the yellow legal pad he kept on his desk and began writing his thoughts of what he might include in his remarks at Danny's funeral. He would be meeting with Charlie and Nora to talk about the service later, and he wanted to have some suggestions prepared to show he was in control. This would be the largest funeral the town had seen in several years. Besides the members of his church, there would be folks in attendance from the community who knew Charlie and Nora, as well as fellow students of Danny's. Extra chairs would probably be needed in the foyer. In spite of his grief, he was a little pleased at the thought of an overflow crowd.

As JD was planning the service, the clock radio on Charlie's bedside table went off just as it had the previous morning. The weather report was similar: heavy fog and cool temperatures. Everything in the world seemed just the same today as yesterday, but everything in his and Nora's lives had been changed forever. Neither of them had slept, really, just dozing off a few minutes at a time, coming to with the feeling that something was terribly wrong before it hit them.

Reaching over to shut off the clock radio, Charlie stared at the ceiling. He had done the same yesterday, before he knew what had happened, and this morning he yearned for that normal world when Danny was still alive. Finally, he forced himself out of bed and got dressed, going through the motions, and headed down to start the coffee.

While the coffee brewed, Charlie walked outside and picked up the newspaper. It was foggy again this morning, and he wondered again how the world was moving on, remembering from yesterday the sound of the sirens. Those police cars had been racing toward Devil's Elbow--the scene of his son's death, and he had been living in a normal world, ignorant of how the world had changed. He looked through the thick fog at the spot where he had assumed yesterday his son's truck was parked. He knew without looking that it was empty today.

Ladner Youth Killed in Crash. "Danny Davis, son of Charlie and Nora Davis, was pronounced dead at the scene of the accident where his truck went through the barricade at Devil's Elbow, located just two miles north of Ladner. Authorities report he died instantly when the truck traveled more than sixty feet and crashed into Cripple Creek. The cause of the accident is still under investigation.

On the obituary page was the picture Nora had given Mickey Thompson. Studying the details of Danny's face, Charlie remembered the moment that picture was taken. Danny's orthodontist had completed Danny's treatment, and as with all his patients, he wanted a picture of the finished product for his before and after records. It was a good way for the orthodontist to show parents what they had paid for, and it had turned out to be a great picture of Danny. Charlie remembered that day perfectly.

Today, Charlie studied every detail of his son's picture: his smile, his eyes, and his hair. It was as though Charlie was looking at a picture of himself at seventeen. *Why couldn't it be my obituary instead of Danny's? A man isn't supposed to bury his child; it goes against the natural order of things.*

He heard Nora coming down the stairs and looked up into her swollen eyes as she slowly shuffled into the kitchen. She noticed the obituaries Charlie held. Sitting down beside him, she took the paper from him, studying the details and quality of Danny's photo. Silent tears ran down her cheeks. Charlie reached for her and drew her head into his neck and shoulder. Together, they wept.

The obituary reported the time and place of the visitation, but Mickey Thompson had asked if they, as a family, would like to see Danny an hour before the visitation began. They agreed to have some private time with their son. The only person who would be present other than their family, would be Sandy.

CHAPTER FIFTEEN

Charlie and Nora walked hand-in-hand into the church. He stopped and put his arm protectively around her. "Are you ready for this?"

Nora closed her eyes and took a deep breath. "In a million years, I could never be ready for this."

JD and Anna were there to meet them and take their coats. Anna looked into her daughter-in-law's face. Anna had already seen Danny, and her eyes reflected a deep sadness at what her son and Nora were enduring.

The lights in the sanctuary were adjusted to a soft, low glow. There was a spotlight above the casket that held Danny's body. Charlie turned his eyes away.

JD pushed open the glass double doors leading into the sanctuary. Soft music was playing; "I Will Meet You In The Morning." Taking a deep breath, Charlie took Nora's arm as they walked down the long aisle toward their son's casket.

JD instinctively knew from his years in the pastorate that soft music soothes and also helps grievers express some of their sorrow.

He had asked the sound technician to line up certain songs that would help them think of heaven.

JD and Anna stood back as Charlie and Nora approached the casket. They recognized this as a private and sacred moment. The two who had brought Danny into the world would now say goodbye to him.

Nora reached out and touched his face. "He looks so handsome and so peaceful. His hair is just the way he likes it." She lovingly ran her hand over the texture of his suit and reached down and straightened his tie, just as she had done many times before.

Nora turned to see Sandy standing with JD and Anna at the back of the sanctuary and motioned her to join them at Danny's casket. Sandy slowly approached and stood between Charlie and Nora. They slipped their arms around her waist and held her as she began to cry. Her cries echoed through the empty sanctuary and soon Nora and Charlie were weeping with her. Anna grabbed some tissues and started to move toward them, but JD stopped her. Years of experience had taught him that this was a needed outlet for their grief, and he didn't want it to be interrupted. Suddenly, JD felt sobs starting to rise in his own chest. He quickly thought of other things, choking them back.

The visitation was scheduled to end at 8 o'clock, but it was nearly 10 when the last person came through the line, hugging JD, Anna, Sandy, Charlie, and Nora. In addition to the visitors from Ladner and nearby towns, there were also relatives who had traveled to Ladner. Charlie was the youngest of JD's and Anna's children and the only son. There were also other grandchildren, and nearly all of them had made the trip.

Most of Sandy's family lived in Ladner. Her mother was nearby; her father and two brothers came through the line and then quickly excused themselves. They would leave Sandy's care to her mother.

When the crowd had thinned out to only a few, JD took charge. "Before we leave tonight, let's gather around the casket for a final prayer." He motioned for everyone to move in closer. "Let's join hands and pray."

JD's voice was solemn and emotional. "Oh God, our hearts are broken by Danny's untimely death. And we know that tonight heaven is much dearer because Danny is there with you right now." Fighting for control, he continued. "So, Lord, help us accept that Danny is in a much better place, and give us the determination to live holy and righteous lives so that we will one day be with him again. Amen."

JD asked Charlie and Nora to walk Anna to their home next door. He would stay and work into the night, planning his remarks for the funeral on the following day.

JD entered the church sanctuary alone and walked slowly to the front.

What can I possibly say to those who will be gathering here tomorrow? He felt his emotions rising. This time, with no one watching, he allowed the sorrow he fought earlier to come out. From his broken heart the deep pain he had suppressed flowed from him. No one was there to comfort him as he wrapped his long arms around himself and rocked back and forth in the pew, crying out his anguish. JD, the pastor who was always in control, cried like a lost and helpless child.

After several minutes, JD dried his tears and slowly made his way back to his office. He shut the door behind him and settled behind the desk in his comfortable black chair. Opening his Bible, he began to give thought to the words he might say at the funeral the following day. He knew this would be the hardest and maybe the largest funeral he had ever conducted. He also knew there would be a large group of Danny's and Sandy's friends from Ladner High. He accurately guessed most of them had never been in a church before. This funeral might be his only chance to preach to these kids, to warn them of the consequences of sin.

He thought about what he wanted to accomplish with his remarks. He wanted to comfort his family by talking about the certainty of heaven. He would no doubt talk about the importance of getting right with God. It seemed to him to be the perfect opportunity to preach about the certainty of death and to evangelize the lost teenagers who would surely be in attendance. He had noticed how emotional they were in the visitation line and was hoping they would return the next day.

It was nearly midnight when JD turned out the light and left the church through the back door, but he had a good idea of what he was going to do. He could see it in his mind's eye. If the funeral went as he hoped, many young people could be saved and filled with the spirit. He smiled and continued to let his thoughts race on. He might even gain some new church members. He needed an infusion of new converts, and Danny's death might be the very thing that would do it. *Maybe,* he thought, *this is why Danny died--to help build his grandfather's church.*

As Charlie and Nora prepared for bed, both of them seemed to be enveloped in a euphoria from what they had experienced during the visitation.

"I can't believe how many people came to say goodbye to Danny and to comfort us." Nora shook her head and looked at Charlie. "I heard such sweet and funny stories about him that I had never heard before."

Charlie nodded. "I know what you mean. One of his coaches told me how the other boys on his team looked up to Danny. He said Danny was a leader and encourager for the other guys. It made me proud. The coach told me he had talked to Danny and told him how much he admired him and how glad he was to have

55

Danny on the team. Danny never even mentioned it to me. I will always be grateful to the Coach for sharing this with me."

They turned back the covers, turned out the lights, and held one another in the darkness. Charlie felt the warm tears of his wife on his shoulder as he held her close. *How will we ever get through tomorrow, God? Help me be strong for Nora.*

CHAPTER SIXTEEN

It had been a sleepless night, but Nora realized she had dozed off when she heard Charlie downstairs making coffee. *Today is the day I will bury my son.* Her thoughts fast-forwarded to Danny's funeral. *What is appropriate to wear to the funeral of one's son? Does it even matter what I wear? Will anything ever matter to me again?*

She knew most of the women attending the funeral would be wearing black, just as she had worn black to the visitation. *I have another black dress in here somewhere,* she thought as she opened her closet door. Her eyes rested on a dress she had bought one day when she had been shopping alone in Springfield. It was pastel blue, and it had been marked down 40 percent. As she ran her fingers over the expensive material, which would ordinarily be out of her price range, she began to justify the expense. Even at 40 percent off, it was more than she felt comfortable spending. *Still, Danny and Sandy would likely be getting married in the next couple of years, so....*

That evening, she decided to show the dress to Danny. She even confided in him that she planned to save it for his wedding—whenever that might take place. She remembered him smiling at her and telling her to keep it handy because he was sure a special occasion would be coming up sooner rather than later. It was a precious memory she would cherish forever.

Deciding to wear this dress would be a bold decision for Nora. She knew there were ladies at church who would be aghast and would be looking at each other and rolling their eyes and wondering what had come over her. She didn't care. She was going to wear this dress to Danny's funeral. And if JD didn't like it, he would just have to get over it.

⇒⇐

At the church, Micah, the custodian, arrived early, turning on the lights, checking the thermostat, and taking care of other details in preparation for the large influx of people who would be in attendance at the funeral services.

Micah was serving time for drunk driving when he and JD became acquainted. JD was holding services for those who were incarcerated and noticed that Micah seemed different from the other inmates. They struck up a friendship, and when Micah got out of jail, he made his way to JD's church and told his story. He had no family, no job, no money, and no place to stay. JD felt compassion toward Micah and was in need of a custodian, so he hired Micah to work at the church 30 hours a week. Micah was a short, wiry guy with multiple tattoos and Brillo-pad hair that stuck out in all directions. But it was the kindness that people saw in his eyes and heard in his voice that disarmed them and caused them to warm up to him.

There were ugly things in Micah's past. He had been abused by his stepfather as a young child and had been on his own since he was 15. He had slept many nights under bridges and in doorways, taking any odd jobs he could find to keep him eating semi-regularly. Soon he found relief from his past memories and present circumstances in alcohol. His life had been hard, and at 37, he looked twice his age.

Micah was thrilled to have this job and felt that working for the church would help him stay close to God—and hopefully God would stay close to him. Each morning when he arrived for work, he went to the altar and knelt to pray and ask God to help him stay sober that day. He was taking it one day at a time, as he had learned in AA, where he had also learned the serenity prayer, *"God, grant me the serenity to accept the things I cannot change, courage to change the things I can, and the wisdom to know the difference."*

This morning, he knelt among the flowers that had arrived for the funeral. Feeling the heaviness of the day, his prayer was exceptionally sincere. When he was a six-year-old child, he had not been allowed to attend his father's funeral. He and his four siblings had been left at home with a babysitter while the grownups drove away to a mysterious and obviously sad meeting. After the adults returned, the children were not allowed to be sad or to mention their dad's name. Micah had tried hard to obey and never talked about him.

Micah had never in his life attended a funeral. When his mother died—a loss that was heavier than the loss of his father—he had not been able to bring himself to attend her funeral. Years later, when he was a husband and father, his wife and infant daughter died during childbirth. Micah didn't attend the service his in-laws had insisted on having. As grandparents and an aunt and uncle passed away, he always feigned an illness that prevented him from going to the funerals. His non-appearance was the topic of much speculation and whispered conversations.

When Micah learned of Danny's visitation and the funeral that would be held at the church, he called the church secretary and told her he had the stomach flu. But when JD learned of Micah's excuse, he let Micah know that he expected him to be there and fulfill his responsibilities or he would be out of a job. No excuses.

So Micah had forced himself to come to work and was committed to doing his very best to overcome the lifelong fear of funerals that had plagued him since he was a kid.

After spending time at the altar, Micah walked down the hallway to the room where the extra chairs were locked away to get started setting them up for the overflow crowd, unaware that Danny's casket had been wheeled into that same Sunday School room after the visitation the night before.

Pulling the master key chain from his pocket, he unlocked the door, stepped into the dark room, and flipped on the light. He froze when he recognized what was before him. The shiny casket triggered memories of his dead father, his mother, his wife and child, and the pain of those losses that he had kept bottled up.

He was swept up into a tornado of sorrow. The color drained from his face, his palms were clammy, and droplets of perspiration appeared on his forehead. He backed out of the room and slammed the door. Stumbling down the hall, he stopped at the water fountain and splashed cold water on his face.

His hands began to shake, and he knew he needed a strong drink if he was going to make it through this day. He looked at his watch and thought he had just enough time to get away to drink some courage and calm his nerves before he faced his duties.

JD was in his office making final touches to his funeral message when Micah left through the back door. Last minute changes had become necessary when JD received a call from his bishop and overseer, Reverend Samuel Jones.

When Bishop Jones heard of Danny's death and that JD was planning to conduct the funeral, he had called JD and offered to drive from Springfield to support JD and his family and to be a pastor to JD during this difficult time. JD had accepted Bishop Jones's kind offer and invited him to read the scripture and pray during the service.

＝≒⁺≒＝

Charlie felt numb as he prepared for the difficult day ahead of him. Reality was a blur to him, and the only reality he could focus on was *Why. Why did Danny drive through the barricade at Devil's Elbow? Why were there no skid marks? Was there something wrong with his brakes? Did he fall asleep?* Aside from the clarity of those tortuous questions running through his mind, he was almost unaware that he was going through the motions of dressing for his son's funeral.

＝≒⁺≒＝

Sandy had spent the long night tossing and turning and weeping. She was out of tears. She gathered up the wet tissues beside her pillow and dropped them in the trash as she made her way to her closet. Sandy was particular about what she wore, and always had her clothes laid out before getting in the shower. But today she was conflicted. Her mom and dad expected her to dress appropriately for the funeral, which meant a dark dress and either conservative or no jewelry.

As she looked at the brightly colored shirts, jackets, and dresses hanging in her closet, it struck her that for a long time she had dressed to elicit an approving smile from Danny. Thinking back to their fun and happy times together, it occurred to her that he often commented that he liked the way she looked in her cheerleading outfit. She remembered thinking that they made quite the pair when she wore that and he wore his letter jacket.

My parents are going to flip, and his grandpa will think I've lost my mind, but that's what I'm going to wear for Danny. I hope his mom is okay with it.

⟫⟪

When Mickey Thompson arrived at the church, he went to JD's office and picked up the key, but when he started to unlock the door, he realized it was already unlocked. He pushed the door open and quickly surveyed the room. Everything seemed to be just as he had left it. He and his assistant carefully rolled Danny's casket down the hallway and into the church sanctuary. As he started to lift the lid of the casket, it occurred to him that he had not asked the family if they wanted the casket to be open or closed for the service. He would keep it closed for now and ask Charlie and Nora what they wanted to do when they arrived.

⟫⟪

JD had been instrumental in designing the church. He met often with the architect as it was constructed, and the platform and pulpit met his specifications. The platform was raised three feet above the floor of the sanctuary and the pulpit was front and center. He wanted to stand above the congregation and be regarded as God's man in charge.

There were three seats on each side of the pulpit, placed back a few feet. The chairs were white, upholstered with red fabric on the seats and backs. The carpet was also red, which signified, JD pointed out, the blood of Christ.

JD felt strongly about the music in his church. He believed the music could make or break a service. He made himself responsible for deciding on each Sunday's special music, believing it was up to him to make certain the force and inspiration of the Holy Spirit was present.

Above and behind the choir loft was a stained glass window that towered 30 feet high and 20 feet wide. The stained glass was constructed and arranged in panes, each one reflecting a meaningful event in the New Testament from the birth of Christ to his death and resurrection. When JD felt pressured or anxious, the life of Christ depicted in the window brought him comfort.

On the left side of the platform was a black grand piano and behind it an elaborate set of drums, all white. JD never allowed the drums to be played during a funeral. He felt that would be out of line and inappropriate. Most of his members felt the same way.

Opposite the piano on the right side of the platform sat a beautiful Hammond organ, and next to it a Leslie speaker. JD believed Hammond organs were a gift from God. He felt doubly blessed that Jane Hill, a member of his congregation, played the Hammond for all services. JD loved the organ because of its strong effect on the crowd during worship, and Jane knew just how to use the settings on the organ to set the desired mood. The unique feature of the Leslie speakers was the horn rotator. The horn had two speeds, and Jane knew how to get the best from each setting.

Jane had gone through a nasty divorce a few years earlier, and JD had a strict policy that anyone who was divorced would not be allowed to be on the platform to take part in a worship service. "It's a bad example to the other couples in my church, and could be construed as approving of divorce."

Once Jane's divorce was finalized and no longer merely "pending," JD faced a dilemma. He had made up his mind to have her dismissed, but the Sunday before he was planning to give her his decision and ask her to resign, things changed.

As JD explained it to his followers, "The church fellowship has experienced such an unusual anointing on the service that

I believe it was a sign from the Lord that Jane should stay on as organist."

From that Sunday on, when JD preached and was "in the spirit," Jane would quietly move from her seat on the front row to the organ. At just the right moment, she would hit the soul-stirring chords, causing a loud response from the boisterous worshippers. It was as though the organ was saying a loud Amen to JD's booming proclamations.

When he asked worshippers to close their eyes and bow their heads, Jane was at her best. JD was a master at telling deathbed stories to prompt sinners to walk the aisle and confess their sins. She played softly for the first few bars of the song, using straight tones. Then, at just the right moment, she pressed the button for the Leslie speakers to kick in with the desired vibrato.

Standing at the pulpit and gazing out over the bowed heads, JD could see the effect of the Hammond on the crowd. He often told church leaders it was like watching the spirit move into overdrive when she performed her musical magic. JD was so impressed by her skills, he had been quoted as saying he had witnessed an avowed atheist weep as Jane worked her magic.

At the back of the church sanctuary were glass walls that extended from the floor up to the top of the thirty foot ceiling. The church had been designed to handle overflow crowds. Chairs could easily be placed in the lobby to accommodate an additional 150 people. There were large speakers in the overflow areas so worshippers sitting in the lobby could hear the service and watch it through the glass partition.

JD had been warned there would be trouble from the fire chief if the sanctuary was full and there were more than 150 in the overflow area, which would exceed the legal seating capacity. Today, he hoped the chief would look the other way. He was certain Danny's funeral would draw the largest crowd ever in his church.

JD had developed a formula for all the funerals he conducted. The family members were directed to a special side room prior to the funeral. This was a time for the bereaved to collect themselves and decide the order in which they would enter the sanctuary. There were times when it was a bit awkward as family members jockeyed for positions at the front of the line. JD's custom was to meet in the side room with the family just prior to the service and have prayer. Then, he would make his way around to the back, near his office and walk out onto the platform to take his seat when Jane clicked a switch that lit a private light in JD's office. Jane was second only to JD when it came to controlling worship and funeral services.

The parking lot was full by 9:45, and drivers were dropping off their passengers at the front door of the church and then going in search of parking spaces on the side streets. Some had to walk several blocks back to the church.

It seemed the whole town had turned out to support the Davis family. There were high school students, young couples with toddlers and carrying infants, as well as senior adults, some using canes or walkers.

Seating for the casket bearers was roped off at the front of the sanctuary. When the entire offensive line of Ladner High School came in, another row of seats was quickly cordoned off. All of the boys were close to six feet tall or taller, with broad shoulders, and they wore their best suits and ties, dressing their best to honor Danny. As a team, they had gone to a local barbershop and had Danny's number, 25, shaved into their hair on the back of their heads. When Nora and Charlie saw what Danny's teammates had done to honor him, they were overcome with emotion.

When Charlie first saw Nora in her blue dress, he was surprised and concerned that she had chosen to wear it to their son's funeral. He knew it would not set well with his dad. JD had very strict standards of what his own family should wear to funerals, and Nora had clearly crossed that line. But as he remembered the occasion that prompted Nora to buy that dress, he recognized what a loving gesture she was making and told Nora she looked beautiful. "Your dress is a loving tribute to Danny, Nora."

Charlie was wearing a dark blue suit, white shirt, blue tie. He wanted to wear something or carry something that would be important to his son. Standing at the kitchen sink, looking into the backyard, Charlie wondered if he too might be able to take something to the funeral, something that would honor Danny. He realized it was standing right in front of him. Spike!

Danny had brought Spike home two years earlier. He had found him abandoned near a construction site and had named him Spike because Danny was driving a spike nail when he first noticed the lonely dog. Fully grown, Spike weighed about 80 pounds and had all the markings of a purebred German Shepherd. He was friendly, and everyone who knew Spike loved him, especially children. Every once in a while Danny could persuade his mother to let Spike into the house, but that was rare. Most of the time he slept in his large dog house in the backyard, not far from the garage.

Danny loved to load Spike in his truck and drive to the park where Spike had lots of space to run and play. Danny taught him to catch a Frisbee and return it for another throw. Danny could throw the Frisbee nearly 75 yards, and Spike eagerly chased it. The big dog would track it down, jump four feet into the air and snag it with his teeth. Danny and Spike usually drew a crowd that applauded each time Spike caught the Frisbee. Sometimes Spike and Danny would be gone for hours, playing Frisbee and entertaining the crowd at the park.

Charlie smiled remembering that Nora objected strenuously when Danny brought Spike home, saying the last thing she wanted was a big dog to look after, because when Danny couldn't feed Spike, the job fell to her. Spike was playful and feisty, often jumping up on her when she went into the back yard to feed him. It was not love at first sight, but soon Nora and Spike became good friends.

Nora noticed Charlie's face as he watched Spike in the back yard, and she read his mind. She wasn't surprised when Charlie said, "I think Danny would want Spike at his funeral."

Charlie headed to the garage to get Spike's leash, and he also grabbed the orange Frisbee, Spike's favorite toy.

When Spike saw Charlie with the Frisbee, he perked up. His trusting eyes touched Charlie's heart as he knelt to hook the leash to Spike's leather collar. Once again overcome with emotion, Charlie leaned his head into the furry neck and cried. The big dog seemed to understand Charlie's mood. He stood still, not moving a muscle.

When Charlie regained his composure, he looked into Spike's eyes, just inches from his face. He whispered, "Help me make it through this day, big boy." Spike cocked his head, then softly licked the salty tears on Charlie's cheeks.

CHAPTER SEVENTEEN

Charlie and Nora arrived at the church and parked in the space that was reserved for them. As they walked through the door, there was not one person who wasn't surprised to see Danny's big dog walking proudly on his leash beside Charlie.

Charlie had grabbed the Frisbee because he thought it would comfort Spike, and he also wanted to include it with the memorabilia that was spread out on the table at the front of the church, which were primarily pictures and other items that were meaningful to Danny.

When Charlie, Nora and Spike entered the church, they felt as though they were in a dream. There were several people standing just inside, their eyes filled with sympathy. Charlie could hardly acknowledge them as they offered their condolences. Spike was on his best behavior. He seemed to understand the importance of the somber occasion.

Bringing a dog to church wasn't completely unprecedented at JD's church. Among the people who had entered the church that day was Sarah Moore, a tiny eighty-seven-year-old lady with severe osteoporosis. She was totally dependent on her walker and needed both hands on it when she walked. Sarah had also lost a child, a depressed son, Michael, who took pills to escape the darkness of his life. Michael had been so severely depressed, his therapist had arranged for a service dog to help him cope with the severe mood swings. It took a while, but he finally got a seventy-five pound lab named Happy, who was specially trained to comfort those who were suffering from severe depression.

JD had initially allowed Michael to bring Happy to church. However, after Michael died, JD strongly objected when Sarah wanted to continue bringing the animal into the sanctuary, even though this same dog, who had brought comfort to Michael, was now bringing comfort to his mother. JD reasoned that Happy had not been medically prescribed for Sarah, and if he allowed one dog in his church, he would have to allow others.

However, after Sarah met with JD privately and made a significant contribution to the benevolence fund, it was decided that Happy could continue attending his church.

Children gathered around Happy every Sunday morning, giving Sarah great joy. The dog was a magnet for adults too. Sarah had even persuaded JD and the photographer to include Happy in the church's pictorial directory

So when Sarah and her dog--with Happy's leash tightly secured to Sarah's walker--arrived for Danny's funeral, the ushers quickly walked them to their favorite spot in the sanctuary.

In his office, JD had given final instructions to Jane Hill as she prepared to start the organ music a few minutes prior to the service. He had given her the list of songs to play as well as the written order of service. She knew all the songs very well; they were the usual funeral songs that just about everyone in attendance would recognize.

JD looked at his pocket watch and realized it would soon be time to start the service, as Mickey Thompson came into his office.

"Excuse me, Pastor, but there is one important thing I almost forgot to ask you about."

"What is it?"

Raising his arms, palms up questioningly, "Do you want the casket open or shut during the service?"

JD pursed his lips. "I think we should keep it closed, but I'll ask Charlie. You'll have time to take care of that prior to the service if he wants it open."

As JD and Mickey made their way to where the family was gathering before walking into the sanctuary together, they could hear Jane playing softly on the Hammond. Nearing the room, JD was stricken by the thought that he was about to conduct his own grandson's funeral. Once again, he reminded himself to put aside personal feelings and move forward with the work at hand.

When JD, the Bishop and Mickey walked in, JD moved close to Charlie and Nora, who were seated. He reached down and gently placed his hand on Charlie's shoulder and whispered loud enough for both Charlie and Nora to hear.

"I need to ask you a last-minute question, son. Do you want the casket open or shut during the service?" JD quickly added, "I told Mickey you would undoubtedly want it closed, but I want to make sure."

Both Charlie and Nora answered immediately. At the same time Charlie said "Closed," Nora said, "Open." JD looked at Charlie and then to Nora, surprised that Nora had spoken up. But her eyes—fiery and determined--cast the deciding vote. JD knew the casket would be open.

JD quickly turned to Mickey and relayed the decision. Out of the corner of his eye, he noticed Spike--and then the orange Frisbee. JD understood why Charlie wanted Danny's dog there, and Charlie had already arranged for one of his young nephews to be in charge of Spike.

Charlie still had the Frisbee in his hand and JD asked, "Would you like Mickey to take the Frisbee up and put it on the table when he goes to open the casket?" Charlie nodded, and handed it to Mickey.

The sanctuary was full and people were being seated in the foyer overflow. Those who had not been to the visitation the night before were lined up to sign the guestbook.

JD took charge of the family room. Clearing his throat and raising his voice, he made his announcements. "There are reserved seats for you in the front of the sanctuary. You should line up behind Charlie, Nora, Sandy, and Anna." Looking around the room, he continued. "I will pray in a few minutes, then Mickey will lead you into the sanctuary to be seated. When the service concludes, you will walk by the casket to say your goodbyes to Danny before he is moved to his final resting place."

As he spoke, a wave of emotion rose up in JD's throat, and he knew it would be dangerous for him to pray at this moment. He turned to the bishop standing nearby. With his voice nearly breaking, he asked, "Reverend Jones, would you kindly pray for me and my family here before we leave this room?"

The little silver-haired bishop turned to the family, and announced, "Let's pray." He prayed a tender-hearted prayer, asking God to watch over the family and to strengthen the grandfather, JD, as he led them in Danny's funeral. He acknowledged that Danny was already in heaven and that this should be a time of rejoicing and not a time of weeping. His prayerful words of rejoicing seemed to be some sort of instruction to the entire family. Nora took note of it and wondered if he had ever lost a child himself. She was pretty sure he had never suffered this kind of loss. She could feel something rising inside of her, a feeling of resentment toward the bishop.

After the prayer, JD hugged Nora and his wife. He nodded to Charlie and made his way, along with the bishop, back to his office where the ministers would await Jane's signal to begin.

The family lined up behind Charlie, Nora, Sandy, and Anna. They moved in two lines, side by side, down the hallway toward the sanctuary. Spike followed obediently behind Charlie and Nora as though he knew what was happening.

There were seventy-eight family members who entered the sanctuary. All eyes were on the procession as it moved slowly down the aisle. Charlie and Nora led the family, walking slightly behind Mickey, as they walked down the aisle, hand in hand. Nora's eyes followed up the long aisle to the front where she saw the profile of her son in the open casket. She held tightly to Charlie as she silently prayed for God to give her strength under the weight of her grief.

Beside Charlie and Nora was Sandy. She wore her cheerleading outfit, short skirt and all. At the last minute, she had asked permission to wear Danny's letter jacket. It was draped around her shoulders as she walked next to Danny's bereaved parents. Nora and Sandy's colorful outfits stood out in contrast to the sea of black that dominated the sanctuary.

Spike had been handed over to twelve-year-old Jimmy, one of Charlie's nephews, who loved playing with Spike when his family visited. Jimmy had been given strict orders to hold on to Spike's leash. If he started barking during the funeral, he was to remove him from the sanctuary as quickly as possible. Jimmy understood and seemed to enjoy his special assignment.

After the family assembled into the assigned pews, Mickey signaled them to be seated. As they sat, one could hear the rattle of Spike's leash as Jimmy positioned himself on the right end of the pew so that Spike could have a place to sit in the aisle. Spike looked up to Jimmy as he motioned with his hand and obediently sat, then stretched out comfortably, his two paws on the carpet cradling his head. He looked straight ahead as though he had been in church many times.

When the small light behind JD's desk began flashing, JD looked at his watch one last time and motioned Bishop Jones to follow. Picking up his Bible, the two ministers walked to the platform and took their seats. Time to begin.

Prior to the service getting started, Micah had returned from the supermarket where he had nervously purchased a large bottle of Jim Beam. He felt totally justified in breaking his sobriety. He ducked back into the side door of the church with the brown paper bag under his jacket, hoping no one noticed. Walking back to the janitor's closet, he stepped inside and closed and locked the door. With shaking fingers, he twisted the cap off the bottle, lifted it to his lips, and savored the sweet hot taste as the magic liquid rushed down his throat. After a good long swig, he closed his eyes and enjoyed the sensation. Satisfied he was now under control, he wiped his lips on his sleeve, put the cap on the bottle, and stuck it under a pile of old drop cloths in a nearby cabinet before rushing out the door to set up more chairs in the lobby. In short order, he felt bolstered by the stiff shot. This was going to be a very tough day, and he was going to do whatever was necessary to get through it.

CHAPTER EIGHTEEN

As Jane played the final chords of "Amazing Grace," JD looked over the heads of the people in the pews as well as those in the outer lobby. He sized-up the crowd so he could measure his words to fit the occasion. That was his specialty. To his left was the assigned family section where Charlie, Nora, and the rest of the family members were seated. To his right he could see the pall bearers, all their sad faces looking straight ahead, none of them moving. Directly behind the pall bearers were about 150 teenagers from Ladner High. JD mentally patted himself on the back for being correct that there would be a large number of students in attendance. This might be his only chance to preach the gospel message to them and hopefully get them saved. He silently prayed God would give a special anointing as he preached.

As the song concluded, JD stood and walked to the pulpit. He allowed his eyes to move toward the open casket in front of him. For a few moments, he couldn't speak as he fought for control of his emotions, wishing Nora hadn't requested the open casket.

Then, as if he had flipped an internal switch, he choked down his emotions and began.

Without looking at the Bible text, JD's voice boomed through the sanctuary. "Hear these words of our Savior, 'I am the resurrection and the life, He that believeth in me shall never die.' Many of you here today are sad because you think that our Danny is dead and gone from us." JD raised his voice to the next commanding level, "Danny is more alive today than he has ever been. He is with the Lord in heaven, a place that is more real than we can imagine. So, we are here today to celebrate Danny's life—not to be sad and sorrowful!"

Forcing himself to smile, JD pointed to his face, "I want you to put a smile on your face, because this is what Danny would want us to do on this day!"

Bishop Jones chimed in with a loud, "Amen," and he was smiling too. Somehow the looks on their faces didn't fit this solemn occasion, but they smiled anyway.

JD had a few more words of admonition. Then, he invited the bishop to read the twenty-third Psalm. The Bishop stepped to the pulpit, opened his Bible and read. He had a smooth and reassuring voice as he read the timeless words, then concluded with a long prayer. As he prayed, Jane played softly on the organ. JD covered his face with his hands in prayer, but he sneaked a peek through his fingers to monitor the congregation, and he could see people wiping tears as they prayed.

After the bishop finished his lengthy prayer, there was a moment of silence. Weeping could be heard throughout the crowd, and even those who were sitting in the lobby, behind the glass walls, were wiping away tears. Holding his Bible, JD stepped back to the pulpit and silently asked God to help him say the words that would get the young people to think about their eternal destinies.

As JD spoke, Charlie held Nora's hand as she bowed her head and silently wept. Deep down he knew there would be no smiling from her, no matter how much his dad wanted everyone to celebrate.

CHAPTER NINETEEN

JD chose to use one of Danny's football games as a metaphor for his sermon. He spoke about the times Danny had carried the ball in the championship game. Many times he had been tackled viciously by the opposing players. He went on to describe how Danny had always gotten up and returned to the huddle to prepare for another play, even though he was hurting. The seasoned preacher knew if he used the football game as an illustration of how the game of life is played, he would have the full attention of the young athletes and cheerleaders that sat before him.

"You are all participants in the game of life, and it is your responsibility to live clean and avoid being tackled by some of the things that could keep you from crossing the goal line and making touchdowns."

Looking directly at the pall bearers, his tone was scolding as he told how drinking, drugs, and pre-marital sex were the enemies of their souls. He made sin out to be the opposing team that tries to tackle and keep one from making touchdowns.

JD spent time describing how these sins have dire consequences, such as drunkenness, addictions, sexually transmitted diseases, and unwanted pregnancies. He didn't leave out a single sin that might touch a teenager's life. This was his big chance, and he wasn't about to waste it.

Pointing his bony finger at the pall bearers, he warned, "There were many times the Blue Devils wanted to tackle Danny in the championship game last October. They would have done it, too, if it had not been for you young men who blocked for Danny and knocked them down. Do you remember that game?" The young players nodded in unison. How could they forget? They recalled it as though it had happened the night before.

JD knew he had their attention. "I was there that night, watching you play that championship game. I was sitting in the last row of bleachers, and I held my breath when the quarterback handed the ball off to my boy, Danny. He bolted through just off the right tackle, then cut back toward the middle of the field." The offensive line hung on every word.

"In all my years of watching my grandson play football, I have never seen such an exhibition of blocking."

JD moved from behind the pulpit to the front of the platform and lifted both hands excitedly. "You men seemed to be everywhere. About the time it looked as though the Blue Devils would tackle my grandson, you knocked them on their butts!"

That was not a phrase JD was accustomed to using from the pulpit, but he was so caught up in the excitement of the story that he forgot his bishop was sitting right behind him. "And I want to tell you this morning that all of us are carrying the ball toward eternity. We need Jesus to knock the devils of hell on their butts so that we can make it all the way to the goal line."

He had them right where he wanted them emotionally, and he was ready to drive home the point.

"Earlier this week, when Danny's truck broke through the barriers at Devil's Elbow, it might seem to you that he was stopped before he reached the goal line."

He paused dramatically before delivering the knockout blow. "But when Danny's truck flew through the air, it wasn't to his death—it was to his eternal life! And when he crossed that goal line last Wednesday morning, he looked up and saw Jesus with his arms raised high in the air, just as the referees raised their hands when he scored that winning touchdown against the Blue Devils."

JD raised his arms to signify a touchdown, and shouted, "Danny made his final winning touchdown, and I think we should give him a hand."

The crowd was so moved by JD's illustration, they had begun applauding even before he told them to. The adults in the crowd agreed with JD's words with their Amens. Charlie was so caught up in the emotion that he stood and clapped his hands as tears streamed down his face. Following that lead, everyone stood.

After the crowd quieted and took their seats, JD walked around to the front of the pulpit and pointed to his lifeless grandson. "What you see here today is the earthly expression of Danny. But, I can tell you on good authority that he has scored the final touchdown of his young life. He is now in heaven, celebrating with Jesus."

He lifted his hand and made a sweeping motion across the sanctuary and asked, "How about you? Do you know for sure that you have Jesus in your heart?" Many of the teens dropped their heads in shame.

"If you were to die this very instant, would you make the final touchdown?" The offensive line was looking at the floor. "The Bible tells us there is a heaven and a hell. Also, there is a great divide--a gulf--between them. All who are with Jesus will be in heaven, but those who do not have Jesus in their hearts will be in an eternal hell where there will be flames, suffering, and eternal separation from their loved ones."

His words lingered in the air for a moment. "I want each of you to bow your head and think what it will be like for you to be separated forever from your loved ones." He shouted the word *forever,* and it reverberated across the sanctuary. While every head was bowed, JD looked toward the organ and nodded to Jane.

As she began to play softly, JD continued working the crowd. "Many of you here today are going to choose the path that leads to destruction. You are the ones who will be suffering and will be eternally separated from your families, from your own mothers. If you don't want to be separated from your families--from your mothers--accept Jesus today and be with them forever."

Now, whispering into the microphone, "You can decide right now and have Jesus blocking out all the Blue Devils of your life. You can invite Jesus into your heart right here, right now."

Jane softly began to play "Tell Mother I'll Be There"; it was JD's favorite for serious altar calls.

The production was having the desired effect.

"If you want to accept Jesus, get out of your seat and walk the aisle and meet me here at the front of the sanctuary. Reverend Jones and I will be waiting here to meet you." This was his moment. He let the soft music play for a few moments and went on, "Walk this aisle, and we will welcome you into the Kingdom of God."

JD and the bishop stepped down to the front and positioned themselves in front of the casket.

Micah stood at the back of the lobby, hanging on to every word. He had made a couple more trips to the storage room and by now was well under the influence of Jim Beam. The alcohol had ramped up his emotions, so when JD invited sinners to come forward to receive Jesus, Micah felt himself moving forward.

Oblivious to his condition, he opened the glass door that separated the outer lobby from the sanctuary and sobbed as he staggered down the aisle, arms lifted high in surrender.

Micah proceeded down the aisle where Spike sat on his leash next to Jimmy, whose head was bowed and whose eyes were closed.

When Micah walked by, Spike stood, shook himself and followed right behind the intoxicated janitor. Jimmy still had his eyes closed and didn't realize what was happening until the leash slipped from his relaxed grip. To his dismay, Spike followed Micah all the way to the front of the sanctuary, dragging the chain behind.

JD also had his head bowed and eyes closed, silently praying. Sensing someone's presence in front of him, he looked up. He recognized the unmistakable smell of whiskey on Micah's breath about the same time he spotted Spike standing with pointed ears and looking at him expectantly.

Micah was clearly under the influence of the wrong spirit. His eyes were closed and his arms were still lifted over his head. His face was turned up toward the stained glass windows, and tears streamed down his cheeks as he half cried and half prayed.

Jane, who had witnessed the scene unfolding before her, took matters into her own hands. As she came to the chorus of "Tell Mother I'll Be There," she hit the setting on the organ console that changed the straight tones to the wave setting.

Something about the sudden change in the organ's tone affected Spike. He cocked his head to one side, and as if in pain, he began to moan in a high-pitched canine groan.

JD was paralyzed. In anticipation of the wave of young people who would be coming forward to confess their sins, he held the holy cup in one hand and a small loaf of bread in the other to offer communion to the converts to seal the deal. Instead of the fresh-faced offensive line, he was surrounded by his bishop, a weeping drunk, and a howling German Shepherd.

He used the hand that held the bread to try and shoo Spike away, but Spike thought he was throwing the bread to be fetched--or eaten--and he bolted off in that direction.

Those seated near the front of the church heard the sudden rattling of the chain and quickly looked up from their prayerful pose. The playful Shepherd rushed under the first row of pews, his big paws gripping the carpet and propelling him toward his treat.

Sitting in the third row was Annabelle McCord, a retired piano player. A very excitable, large woman with a tender disposition, Annabelle had cried during most of the service. Her eyes were still closed when Spike ran under the pew and between her legs.

When the furry animal ran under her, Annabelle let out a blood-curdling scream that was heard in not only the sanctuary but the overflow area as well.

Happy, the other canine guest, was stretched out on the floor when she was awakened by Annabelle's scream. Suddenly she saw the big Shepherd coming toward her at full speed. The black Lab scrambled to her feet with a quick bark of warning.

Before a human could react, both dogs were on their hind legs, snapping and biting; Annabelle was still shrieking in the background.

The moment of mass salvation had deteriorated so quickly that no one knew what to do. Spike, the heavier of the two, seemed to be winning. Then Happy sunk her teeth into Spike's neck, causing him to yelp with pain and hastily retreat back toward the altar where the flowers were on display. Happy gave chase, dragging Sarah's walker behind her.

Spike darted between a large bouquet of gladiolas from the Methodist congregation and the roses from Buck's. Happy, still angrily giving chase, was close on his heels with Sarah's walker tumbling along behind. When the dogs ran past the casket, Sarah's walker hit the two baskets of flowers along with six other nearby arrangements, creating an explosion of colorful flowers, water, and vases that doused the front row with splashing water and flying blossoms.

Suddenly, Happy's walker was snagged in the railings of the altar, preventing her further pursuit of Spike. She resorted to jumping and tugging on her leash and barking ferociously. Spike, safely on the other side of the church, turned and barked back. After realizing Happy was no longer in pursuit, Spike bravely ventured back and stood just three feet out of Happy's reach and continued barking indignantly.

In thirty seconds, the mood of the service was changed.

Amid the chaos, Charlie thought of the Frisbee. He retrieved it from the table where it was displayed and waved it in front of Spike, then hurled it toward the back of the sanctuary. Forgetting all about Happy, Spike bounded toward the door and snagged the Frisbee, with Charlie right behind him. Later, Charlie thought back on what happened and smiled, enjoying that Danny's dog had played such a prominent part in the funeral, even though it was unplanned.

Once the dogs were removed from the sanctuary, JD demanded that Micah clean up the mess, and Mickey hurriedly began dismissing people, row by row. Not everyone chose to pass by the casket again, but those who did stepped carefully around the overturned baskets of flowers.

When the church was nearly empty, Mickey motioned to Charlie and Nora and the rest of the family to come forward before he closed the casket. Charlie and Nora studied the curve of his neck, the contour of his nose and lips, the color of his hair. They knew they would never forget—and they would never be the same.

Charlie turned to Mickey as he prepared to close the casket. "Could you give us just a few more minutes?"

"Sure, Charlie, whatever you want."

Charlie walked to the front door and found Jimmy holding Spike on his leash just outside the door. Charlie took the leash and led the dog back inside to the front of the altar.

"Here boy, you can say goodbye too."

Spike rose up on his hind leg and put his front paws on the edge of the casket and peered inside. He made a soft whining sound before he took his eyes off Danny's face and looked expectantly at Charlie. It was hard for Nora and Charlie and the other close family members to watch Spike say goodbye to Danny.

Danny's offensive line easily lifted his casket and carried him out of the church. The two ministers led the procession toward the cemetery and to the spot where Danny would be buried.

When the family gathered around the grave, Charlie, Nora, Sandy, and Anna sat on the front row of chairs. JD stepped to the head of the casket and read from his Bible, "Let not your hearts be troubled; ye believe in God, believe also in me. In my father's house are many mansions. If it were not so, I would have told you. And if I go and prepare a place for you, I will come again and receive you unto myself, that where I am, there ye may be also." Then he led the group in praying The Lord's Prayer.

Charlie stood and turned to the group of mourners gathered there. "Nora and I want to thank you for being here with us today. Your love and support has been more than we could have imagined. We don't know how this happened or even exactly what happened, and we feel that the life of our precious son has been snatched away from us. We feel cheated right now. Please remember to pray for us. Right now, we don't know how we're going to move on from this loss." As he spoke, Nora sat looking straight ahead at the metallic blue casket.

CHAPTER TWENTY

E arly the next morning, the clock radio came on at the usual time. Charlie got up and made his way downstairs and started the coffee before going outside to retrieve the Sunday paper. As he glanced through the news of the day, he noticed an article about another accident that involved a young girl in a nearby town. She, also, had been in a pickup, and had lost control of it after a blow-out. The truck veered off the road, hit a mailbox, and rolled over twice. She had walked away barely scratched.

Charlie felt cheated as he read the newspaper article. He especially noticed that she gave credit to her guardian angel who had watched over her that night. *Where was Danny's angel three nights ago?* Charlie slammed the paper on the kitchen table in disgust. *Why did God spare that girl's life and let Danny die? God, it isn't fair!*

For the next week, Charlie and Nora stayed at home. Each day, more sympathy cards appeared in their mail box. By actual count, they opened and read more than two hundred. Some were carefully worded notes of condolence, others were scripture quotes about heaven, assuring them they would see Danny again one day.

Some suggested Danny's death would be a blessing to others if Charlie and Nora surrendered his death to the will of the Lord. Most of the cards with Bible-verse messages were from members of their church who hoped scripture would help answer the question of why Danny had died. They wanted Nora and Charlie to understand that there must be a reason for it.

There were practical matters that needed Charlie's and Nora's immediate attention, and near the top of that to-do list was going to the high school and clearing out Danny's locker. The principal had called and asked how they wanted to handle it, and Charlie and Nora decided they preferred to go after school was out for the day and the students gone. They made arrangements to meet in the principal's office that afternoon. Charlie found a box in the garage that he thought would be of adequate size to hold Danny's things. He suggested to Nora that he go alone to take care of it. By this time, Nora couldn't go even an hour without breaking down, and he thought it might be too much for her, but she was adamant that she wanted to go with him.

When they met Mr. Sturgis, the principal, in his office, he also offered to gather the belongings from Danny's locker and deliver them to the house, but Charlie assured him it was something they wanted to do themselves. Holding the master key in his hand, Sturgis led the way down the empty hall toward the student lockers.

The bereaved couple were deeply touched by the evidence of the students' affection for Danny as they approached his locker. There were flowers everywhere. Red and pink roses, along with carnations too. Among the flowers were small envelopes and pieces of paper on which students had written messages they had either taped to the door of Danny's locker or left on the floor in front of it.

"I had no idea the students did this," Sturgis said. "No one told me. I'm sorry you had to see this."

Nora was barely able to speak, "Oh, no, don't apologize. We love it."

Sturgis stepped over and slipped the key into the lock but didn't open the door. "Do you want me to stay here with you or..."

"If you don't mind, we will do this by ourselves," Charlie said.

The principal understood. He turned and walked toward his office, the sound of his shoes echoing down the empty hallway.

Nora knelt down and tenderly gathered the flowers and put them in the box. Charlie carefully peeled off the tape that held the messages to the door. As Nora was picking up the long-stem flowers, she noticed something that caught her eye. There was a special long-stem rose with a small rosebud attached to it. She didn't see the rosebud until she picked up the rose and noticed the bud tucked down inside the floral paper. She had seen an identical rose and rosebud arrangement among the flowers at the funeral. It seemed odd and out of place--like a mistake maybe--but she lovingly put it in the box.

After collecting the messages and the flowers, Charlie pulled on the door to the locker; it squeaked as it came open. Inside, one of Danny's hoodies hung on the hook, and on the top shelf were his books. Under the books was a notebook marked up with some of his doodling. He had tried to draw some of the NFL logos, but it was easy to see that art was not his thing. In the bottom of the locker was an assortment of his belongings. His ball glove and bat were there, ready for baseball season to begin. Two pairs of shoes were squeezed in: his spikes and some ratty tennis shoes. Nora had asked Danny to throw those shoes out; apparently, he couldn't bring himself to do it.

Fastened to the inside of the locker door were his class schedule and a calendar that had each day of the month with an X through it right up to the day he died. There was a 3 X 5 picture of Sandy in her cheering outfit, announcing, "All my love forever." Nora carefully took each item and placed it in the cardboard box.

When Charlie closed the locker door and they started back down the hall, he vowed he would not come to this school again. Retrieving his son's belongings had been one of the most painful things he had ever experienced.

CHAPTER TWENTY-ONE

The next morning, Charlie mentioned he was thinking about going back to work.

"I thought I might go to the shop for a while today and see if I'm up to it. Maybe I will go back for just a few hours a day to start.

Nora didn't think she would ever be ready to face the world again, but she knew Charlie would have to go back to work at some point. "If you think you can do it, go ahead."

The following morning, Angie noticed Charlie from her office window as he walked slowly toward the shop from where he parked his truck across the street. *Lord, help him. He looks so sad and defeated.*

When Charlie walked through the door, he breathed in the familiar pungent odor of oil and gasoline and heard the comforting sound of an impact wrench. Pat was putting a tire back on a car and finishing a brake job. This was Charlie's world, a place that felt comfortable and predictable; nothing like the miserable chaos of the last several days.

As Pat finished tightening the last lug nut on the wheel and snugging it down with his impact wrench, he turned and was shocked to see Charlie walking toward his workbench.

Setting on top of his tool box in his work bay was an arrangement of flowers with a note attached. "We are so sorry. We loved him too." It was simply signed, "From your friends in the shop and office." As he had done many times every day for the last week, Charlie fought back tears.

He had been working on an engine overhaul when he last left the shop. There were parts and pieces of the engine all over his bench as well as the surrounding floor and nearby shelves. The pistons, rings, engine head, oil pan, bolts, nuts, carburetor, air cleaner, brackets of all sorts, were just as he had left them. The engine had been torn apart and he had been just about ready to put it all back together again. If today was just another day, he knew he would tackle a job like this and have the engine back together before quitting time. But everything seemed different today. He stood looking at the scattered parts and pieces of the engine and thought how much his life resembled the scattered car parts. Danny's death had left him in pieces. He feared he might never find the missing parts, let alone put them together again.

No one approached Charlie; they didn't know what to say. Finally, after a few minutes, Pat went to the coke machine and bought two Cokes, one for himself and one for Charlie. With a can in each oily hand, Pat strolled over, just as he so often did during their mid-morning breaks. He held out one of the Coke's to Charlie. "Hey, man, could you use one of these?"

Charlie accepted the can, "Thanks, buddy, but do you have anything stronger than this?" He was half-smiling in an attempt to put Pat at ease.

Pat leaned back against the car in Charlie's bay. "I didn't expect you back so soon. I thought maybe I would come back in tonight, after the shop closed, and put your engine back together." Pat nodded toward the scattered parts as he spoke.

Charlie took a good long drink and wiped his mouth with his sleeve. "Thanks, Pat, but I can probably handle it now. I just wanted to slip in and see how things were going. I might go out back and take a look at Danny's truck, too. Is it still there?"

Pat nodded and offered to go with him. They walked through the shop and out the back door.

"Do you have any idea what happened or why he missed that turn, Charlie?"

Charlie shook his head.

"Here, Pat. Will you hold this for a minute?" As he handed his drink to Pat, he dropped down to crawl under the truck.

Charlie scooted himself up under the rear end of the truck, not caring about the dirt he was grinding into his clothes. He was looking at the brakes, thinking there might have been a problem no one else had detected. The police had told him there were no skid marks on the road to indicate the brakes were applied before Danny went through the barrier.

Charlie remembered Danny's brakes had been repaired by Vern Collins just a week or two before the accident. Vern was the newest hire in the shop, and he had offered to do the brake job in exchange for Charlie tuning up his vintage Chevy.

Charlie wondered if Vern had missed something. He examined both the rear brakes as best he could, paying careful attention to the brake linings, but found nothing wrong. He couldn't look at the front brakes; the front of the truck was too badly damaged.

CHAPTER TWENTY-TWO

C harlie spent the rest of the week with Nora. Late Saturday night, she announced she was not going to church the next morning.

"I'm not ready to face anyone at church. I know JD won't like it, but I don't care. I'm not going."

The next morning, after a couple cups of coffee, Charlie decided he would try to make it through the worship service alone.

He could feel people watching as he nodded to the greeter and quickly slipped into a vacant seat in the last pew.

JD had ordered lively and upbeat praise music for the morning. He wanted to help the worshippers get their minds off Danny's death, so each chorus they sang was a hand-clapping, fast-tempo tune to raise their spirits. Jane's fingers moved quickly over the Hammond organ's keyboard, and the pianist, drummer, and other instrumentalists rocked the crowd with their loud music, their faces showing how much they enjoyed being turned loose.

JD usually did not stand during the worship music. He reasoned he needed his energy for his sermon. He sat still, sizing up the worshippers as they clapped and sang. He looked back and saw Charlie and nodded, indicating he was pleased to see him in church, even though Charlie wasn't singing. He hadn't expected to see Nora.

JD's sermon was from Paul's words to be "thankful in every-thing." He decided that his congregation might be thinking if tragedy could happen to the pastor's grandson, it could happen to them too. So, he felt it was an opportunity for him to lead the way in giving thanks and praise to God, even for Danny's death. The music sung earlier carried the same theme.

JD told a funny story Charlie had heard many times, but it kept Charlie distracted for a while. His eyes kept wandering back to the window through which he could see the fresh dirt mounded over his son's grave. *Will there ever be a day I don't think about it?* Charlie left before the altar call and his dad's final prayer.

CHAPTER TWENTY-THREE

Nora had cried most of Sunday, and when Monday morning came, Charlie drank his coffee, took a quick look at the paper before kissing her goodbye and headed to the Boar's Head.

The waitress and cook were surprised to see him, as were Tom, Al, and Tiny. As Charlie took his usual place, his three friends turned sideways on their seats. They couldn't miss the grief that dominated his face, and none of them knew what to say.

"You having your usual this morning, Charlie?" He nodded in response, and Maria turned to tell the cook.

Charlie quickly sensed the awkwardness of the moment and tried to put his breakfast companions at ease. "I saw you all there at the funeral. Thanks for coming."

"Don't mention it, it's the least we could do. We're sorry about what happened."

Charlie sensed the sincerity. But, he wanted things to be as they were before--before the accident.

Charlie gave them a slight smile. "What did you guys think of the dog fight that broke out?"

It was silent for a moment. Then, everyone laughed out loud, and it broke the ice.

Tom raised his coffee mug and grinned. "Tiny and I saw the whole thing from where we sat. When it started, I turned to Tiny and whispered, 'Man, my money is on Spike. I'll bet you five dollars he can take that lab!"

Charlie laughed. "I like that you bet on Spike, but I think the whole thing ended in a draw. Danny would have loved it!"

Charlie finished eating, paid his bill, and headed to work. *It'll feel good to get back to my routine. Work will help me get my mind off things.*

As he started working, it didn't take him long to realize there were several engine parts he would need to finish the job. He found the work order, studied it again, and made notes on the parts he needed. He was having a hard time concentrating, and he had to look at a part number repeatedly before writing it down. When he finally made it to the parts counter, he had to go back three more times. His mind wasn't working well, and he knew the parts manager noticed it too. Simple tasks seemed challenging, and he felt like a novice mechanic.

About 10:30, Angie came out to Charlie's work stall. He was on a creeper under the car he was repairing.

Angie leaned down and whispered, "Charlie, I just had a phone call from Nora, and it sounds urgent. She wants you to call her as soon as you can." He slid the creeper out and reached for a shop rag, wiped off his hands, and followed her to the office.

"Charlie, I need you to come home...now," and she hung up.

Charlie turned to Angie. "I need to go home. Will you let Buck know? I'll be back just as soon as I can."

When Charlie got to the house, Nora was at the kitchen table in her robe; her hair was a mess. Her eyes were red and puffy, and she was wadding tissues in her hands.

"Charlie, I can't do this alone." She buried her head in his shoulder. "People keep calling. The insurance adjustor wants to meet with us. The monument salesman wants to know when we are going to choose a permanent marker. And Mickey wants to know how many death certificates we will need. I can't do this! Every time the phone rings it has something to do with Danny's death. I need you to help me with all of it."

"Whatever you need, honey. Whatever you need."

Charlie wondered how long this intense suffering would continue. He realized the grief was still very fresh, but he felt things might never get back to normal. Danny's death was starting to settle in on his mind, but he felt an unusual sense of fear for the future—and for himself and Nora as a couple.

Over the next few days, they met with the insurance adjuster, decided on the number of death certificates, and chose a permanent marker for Danny's grave.

Going to the cemetery office to choose the monument for Danny's grave was a difficult and costly process. When the purchase was completed, Charlie realized it was last thing they could do for their wonderful son. Nora was barely able to hold herself together as they left the office. When they got back in their car, Charlie reached over and put his arms around her. He could feel her body shaking as she sobbed. Feeling her pain, Charlie felt the tears rush to his own eyes, and this time he could not hold them back. They streamed down his face and onto the collar of Nora's coat. He made no sounds of crying, and she could not feel the dampness of his tears through her coat. He didn't want her to see his emotions. He wanted to be strong for her.

After several minutes, he started the car and drove slowly through the cemetery. They had not planned it, but it seemed natural to drive up the narrow road that led to Danny's grave.

As they got nearer, they saw a parked car, and as they got nearer still, they recognized the car as Sandy's. Charlie pulled up behind her car, and they could see her sitting alone inside it. From behind, it appeared that her head was down on the steering wheel.

Nora asked Charlie to give her a minute and quickly got out of the car while Charlie stayed inside. He watched as Nora approached the driver's side window. She pecked on the window and Sandy lowered it, and she and Nora talked for a moment. Then, Nora returned to Charlie.

"She's having a really hard time, Charlie, and I want to spend some time with her. She said she'll drop me off at the house. I'll be okay."

"You sure?"

"Yes, I'm sure. It will be good for us to have a few minutes together." She leaned in and gave Charlie a peck on his cheek. As Charlie drove away, Nora walked to the passenger side of the car and opened the door. Sandy was trying to get her school books out of the seat and into the back.

"Looks like you were doing some studying today."

Sandy wiped her eyes and said softly, "I just couldn't focus at school today. I went to the counselor's office and asked if I could be excused." Sandy looked toward Danny's grave, barely able to talk, "The counselor seemed to know why I needed to get out of school. Every time I go to my locker, I see Danny's face, and today there are more flowers and notes at his locker. Mrs. Davis, I don't know if I can live without Danny."

Nora reached down and put her hand on Sandy's, "I know, honey. All our lives are changed forever."

When they finally wiped their tears away and settled back into their seats, their eyes turned toward Danny's grave. Baskets of flowers were turned on their sides, banked up against the mound of dirt over his grave. The white gladiolas were brown and wilted, as were the carnations and roses. Nora thought the wilted flowers represented their lives. But somehow it comforted her to be close to Sandy. In a strange way that Nora couldn't understand, Sandy was her connection to Danny.

Sandy turned to Nora and began to share her feelings. "All my life I have been able to earn extra credit in my classes if I needed to fix something I had missed earlier, but there is nothing I can do to fix this."

Nora nodded. She knew exactly how Sandy was thinking and feeling. Nothing, absolutely nothing, could bring back her son or Sandy's sweetheart.

They sat in silence, looking out across the cemetery. They held hands, each remembering the happy times when they were all together.

"Sandy, did you know Danny was planning to propose to you at Christmas?" Sandy caught her breathe and Nora felt her small hand tighten under hers.

"Well, no, I didn't know he was going to do it at Christmas."

"He told me one night when just the two of us were together. I never told Charlie, and I doubt Danny told him either. Danny and I had a few secrets, and that was one of them. After he told me, I started a little Hope Chest in the spare bedroom. I bought a few baby things whenever I found something special--some for a baby boy and some for a little girl." Nora looked out again toward Danny's grave.

"I probably shouldn't tell you this, but I secretly hoped you and Danny would get married. The two of you would have brought us some grandbabies to love. I so wanted to be a grandmother, but now...."

Sandy heard the despair in Nora's voice. They sat together quietly, each remembering her own dreams for a future that included Danny.

CHAPTER TWENTY-FOUR

Leaving the cemetery, Charlie decided to stop by the shop. When he walked in, he noticed immediately that the engine overhaul he had been working on was nearly finished. When he saw what Pat and the others had done, he felt an overwhelming sense of gratitude.

Pat was making final adjustments on the carburetor and came out from under the hood, wiping his hands on a greasy shop rag. He saw Charlie and motioned toward the car as he spoke, "Just thought we would give you a hand here. I hope you don't mind."

"Mind? I don't mind at all, and I can't believe you guys did this for me."

Pat walked to the workbench and picked something up and held it up for Charlie to see. "Look at this. This explains why the engine needed an overhaul. I looked at the oil sticker, and the oil and filter should have been replaced forty thousand miles ago. Can you believe it?"

Pat rolled his eyes and shook his head. "I guess he just ignored oil changes and thought everything would be okay. I have known the owner for a long time, and it's just like him to try to save some money by not keeping up with the maintenance. Now, it's going to cost him a bundle, probably more than a thousand bucks when all is said and done."

Pat motioned for the other mechanics within earshot to see what he had discovered and why the engine overhaul was necessary.

"Charlie, when this guy comes to pick up his car, show him this dirty filter. Explain to him that this is what happened because he didn't do preventive maintenance. Hold it up and let him see the sludge that clogged his engine. This whole problem was caused by neglect."

Pat turned off the shop light, pulled the cloth off the fender, and gently closed the hood.

I think she's ready for a test drive, Charlie.

Charlie nodded, grabbed a shop fender cover and spread it out over the driver's seat. He slid behind the wheel, revved the engine a little so they could hear the sound of it. Then they smiled at one another in approval.

Charlie headed out in the direction of his Dad's church. He planned to take his usual test-drive route that started from the edge of the church property. When he got there, he checked his mirrors and hoped no one else was around; he wanted to hear how the car sounded when he got it up to speed.

As he drove past the church sign and the cemetery, he saw that Sandy's car was still parked there.

Charlie pressed down on the accelerator and felt the car take off just as he hoped it would. He didn't want to drive too fast; that wouldn't be good during the break-in period of a newly over-hauled engine.

He was driving on the stretch of road that Danny had been on the night of his death. It had been late, and it was foggy. *What happened? If it wasn't the brakes, what caused Danny to drive through the barrier? If only I could have examined the master cylinder and seen*

100

the condition of the brakes. For the umpteenth time, he mulled over every possible reason for the accident and the ways it might have happened.

His eyes filled with tears, and he pulled to the side of the road and sat there a few minutes with the engine running. A guy in an old black pickup rumbled by him going in the same direction. A plume of blue smoke curled out the back of the exhaust. Charlie could smell it. *He needs a ring job. Probably another one of those guys who thinks he can get away with not taking care of his engine.*

Charlie was just a quarter mile from Devil's Elbow, and he could see it off in the distance. He turned the truck around and headed back to the shop; he didn't intend to ever drive to Devil's Elbow again.

When he got back to the shop, his Dad was waiting for him.

JD rarely came to the shop unless he was having trouble with his car, and Charlie could tell by the look on his dad's face this was not a social call.

"Hey, Dad, good to see you. What brings you here?"

"Charlie, can I talk to you?" He motioned toward the back of the shop and started walking in that direction. They walked through the back door near the area where Danny's wrecked truck was parked.

"I came here for a couple reasons, son. I want to see the truck again and ask if it has been examined carefully." JD emphasized the word carefully."

"Daddy, I examined the brakes in the back myself, and, as you can see, we can't determine what the front ones look like."

JD put one hand on the tailgate, looked in the bed of the truck, and pointed. "How do you think *those* got in there?"

Charlie moved close. "What do you mean?"

JD reached over the tailgate, pointing to some objects in the corner of the truck bed. Crumpled up, almost out of sight, were empty beer cans that had been mashed down and pitched into the bed of the truck.

"Tell me the truth, Charlie. Did you know he had been drinking?" JD's voice was loud and condemning.

"I haven't seen those in there before. He told me that he tried beer a couple years ago but that he didn't like it, and he told me that on his own accord. I've never smelled liquor on him and neither has Nora. I don't know how those got in there, and I don't think they're his. Anybody could have thrown them back there since the truck has been parked here a while."

"Everyone who knows me knows how I feel about alcohol. I would hate to think that my own grandson had been drinking when he crashed his truck. But we'll let that go for now. That isn't what I came to talk to you about. I came to talk to you about Nora."

"What about her?"

"Well, as you know, I can see Danny's grave through my office window."

"Yeah, I know."

"I saw Sandy and Nora out there today. They sat there a long time. You and I both know what they were doing."

"Yes, I know. I was there for a while myself."

"Well, son," JD went on, "I want to give you some fatherly advice, and I hope you take it from your old dad in a good way. You need to nip this stuff in the bud right now. If you don't, Nora will be out there, crying over Danny, every day."

JD raised his voice again and gestured in the direction of the cemetery. "I've seen some women going there every day for years to sit by their child's grave and cry. A pastor friend of mine told me that he had a lady in his church who crawled over the fence at night after they locked the gates to sit by her child's grave."

JD's face was stern. "Son, you and I both know it won't do Nora any good to keep moping around about what happened to Danny. I'm sad too, but we can't allow her or ourselves to be paralyzed by grief over Danny's death. We all need to move on--Nora, you, Anna, even me."

He kicked at the caked mud on the edge of the tire and continued. "You know the women's group at church have that conference in Kansas City starting in a few days. Nora signed up to ride the bus up there with the other women before Danny died. I doubt you realize it, but the theme of that conference is, 'Providers of Joy.' This can be a life-changing experience for the women who go up there if they mind the Lord and get into the spirit of it. This event could be the place of a Holy Ghost revival, and it could even result in a great spiritual renewal in our church." JD's eyes sparkled with the possibilities.

"But if Nora gets on the bus with that sad face and all of the women see her crying, well, you can just imagine what it will be like for the women riding to Kansas City with her. I'm deeply concerned, and I think you had better do something about it."

JD was oblivious to the stunned look on Charlie's face. "After all, if this sad sack stuff continues on much longer, it will simply turn into self-pity. To tell you the truth, I think she is getting pretty close to that already. And if I discern the scriptures correctly, St. Paul commands us to give thanks to God for *all* things.....*all* things, son."

JD looked at the ground and shook his head. "I don't understand why Danny was snatched away from us, son. But I do know God loves for us to praise him in every circumstance that life throws our way. The scriptures declare to us how God inhabits the praise of his people! Do you understand me, son?"

Charlie nodded numbly. His dad wanted him to fix Nora--and soon.

"I'll see what I can do, Dad. But it isn't going to be easy to get Nora to come around. I can't guarantee you're going to get the results you're hoping for."

CHAPTER TWENTY-FIVE

Charlie was still feeling the pressure of the talk with his dad when he walked in the door and found Nora wrapped in Danny's robe. He could tell she had been crying.

"Why are you wearing Danny's robe?"

Nora held the robe more tightly around herself and lifted her chin defiantly. "It helps me feel closer to him."

"Nora, this isn't helping you."

"I don't expect you to understand this, Charlie. I just miss him so much, I will do anything and everything I can to feel closer to him."

Charlie walked over and took her in his arms. Looking up to the ceiling, he closed his eyes and silently prayed, Oh, God, please get her through this-- soon!

Later, Charlie asked Nora if she was hungry.

"No, but I know you think I need to eat."

"Why don't you get dressed and I'll take you to Sam's Steakhouse."

Nora was wary, but she agreed, thinking it might be good to get out of the house. She forced herself to get ready.

Sam's Steakhouse was a nice place to celebrate special events. Birthday parties, anniversary celebrations, and even wedding receptions were often held at Sam's. With white tablecloths on the tables and cloth napkins, it was a big step up from the Boar's Head.

When they walked in, Charlie asked if they could have a corner booth, hoping for some privacy. Nearly everyone in town knew about Danny's death, and Charlie didn't want to run into people who would feel compelled to tell them how sorry they were. It was awkward when others didn't know what to say, and Charlie found it exhausting to try and put them at ease. He knew Nora couldn't hold up if they were put in that position.

Nora took the seat facing away from the door when they were shown to a table. Charlie asked the waitress for water and coffee, while Nora asked for hot green tea.

When it was time to order, Charlie asked for a steak, complete with a salad and French fries. Nora would settle for a salad and baked potato.

After they were served, Charlie noticed that Nora was picking at her potato and had forced down only a couple bites.

"Aren't you going to eat?"

Nora put her fork down. "Charlie, I just can't eat. And, please, don't try to force me to do something I don't want to do."

"So, do you want me to take you back home?"

Nora picked up her coat and started to slide out of the booth. It was obvious to Charlie she was irritated with him.

As she started to get up, she came face to face with Martha Goins and her husband who were on their way to one of the private rooms. They were dressed up and on their way to the special banquet room in the back of the restaurant.

"Nora, it is so good to see you. I was so sorry to hear about Danny."

Nora flinched, looked down at the floor, and responded softly. "Thank you, Martha. It looks like you're celebrating something special tonight."

Martha shot a side glance at her husband. "Our daughter, Sally, just announced her engagement to the Harris boy, so we're here to help the kids celebrate."

Nora forced a smile. "Oh, Martha, I think that is so wonderful for them--and for you. You must be very happy." Nora hugged the happy mother of the bride.

There was a quick goodbye as Charlie and Nora left. When they arrived at the car, Charlie opened the door for her and went around, got in on the driver's side, and slipped the key into the ignition. He sat there a moment without starting the engine, then looked at Nora. "Why can't you give me some of that?"

"What are you talking about?"

"Well, just two minutes ago, you heard Martha's good news, and you gave her a glowing smile. I haven't seen you smile in a long time. Why can't you smile at me once in a while?"

"Charlie, they're celebrating a very special occasion. I was just trying to be supportive, even though...even though...." Her voice trailed off, and she could barely whisper. "Even though we will never get to have a party like the one they are having."

"I was hoping to have a nice dinner here, go home and spend some special time together—like we used to."

Nora looked straight ahead.

"I had a long talk with Daddy today, Nora. He noticed how long you and Sandy stayed at the grave.

"And just what's so wrong about me spending time at our son's grave?"

"Well, Dad and I feel this is just making you feel sadder and--well, it just doesn't look good for the pastor's daughter-in-law to look so sad all the time. You've heard Dad preach that truth many times. He said it again not long ago. We, as Christians, are supposed to give thanks to God in all circumstances, to express the joy of the Lord through our praise and worship." He hesitated. "Even when our hearts are breaking."

Nora wondered if she had heard him right.

"Nora, in just a few days the ladies ministry is taking a bus up to Kansas City to the national women's conference--'Providers of Joy.' You already paid to go, and Daddy is concerned about you getting on the bus with that sad look on your face. And, I think he is right. If you get on there and cry all the way to Kansas City, you will ruin it for everyone else who wants to receive a blessing."

Nora's face was flushed with anger at her husband and her father-in-law. She looked straight ahead through the windshield, her teeth tightly clenched.

"Take me home, Charlie. Now."

CHAPTER TWENTY-SIX

Charlie soon went back to his regular work schedule, but Nora was still not putting on a happy face for him or anyone else. She rarely went to church, didn't cook, and didn't care much about the way she or the house looked.

Although Anna's tendency was to cut Nora some slack, JD thought she was in a downward spiral, and Charlie agreed. JD called or went by to see Charlie every day. In his estimation, Nora was a poor example of what a model Christian should be.

Most evenings, at 5 o'clock, Charlie walked across the street to the Boar's Head to get something to eat, then went back to the shop and worked until 8. It was painful to be with Nora, and he was beginning to avoid going home to his wife.

Deep down, Nora knew Charlie was unhappy. There was no doubt their marriage was suffering and probably on the brink of falling apart.

She recalled an occasion before Danny's death when her cousin told her about a Christian counselor in Springfield who had helped her and her husband work through some problems in their marriage. Nora decided she would bring it up to Charlie. She called her cousin to get the number of the counselor.

When she first mentioned marriage counseling to him, Charlie thought it was a bad idea--especially when he found out how much each session was going to cost. Nora was determined and very persistent, though, so Charlie gave in and Nora called and made the appointment.

It was a quiet drive to Marcia Moore's office in Springfield on the Friday afternoon of their first appointment. Ms. Moore was a certified, licensed, marriage therapist with an office located in an older downtown building.

The middle-aged receptionist looked up and smiled from behind her glass-partitioned office when they walked through the door that led to the suite of offices. She slipped open the window and handed Nora a clipboard and asked that she and Charlie fill out the forms prior to meeting with Marcia.

The form requested the usual contact information and the name of the person responsible for payment. On the back, Nora and Charlie were asked to give family and background information.

Charlie read down the list of questions that asked not only for his personal history but also for the personal histories of his mother and father. He shifted uneasily in his seat when he saw the questions related to substance abuse and addictions. He knew of his dad's alcoholism but decided that information was none of the counselor's business.

Almost immediately after they finished their paperwork, they were led to Marcia's office to meet the counselor. She appeared to be in her early forties and her voice was welcoming and gentle. She took their forms and invited them to take seats in a simple arrangement of padded armchairs, all three facing at a comfortable distance apart.

After studying their forms for a few minutes, she offered them coffee or water, motioning toward the coffee pot that had nearly a full pot of freshly brewed coffee in it. Nora asked for a cup of water and Charlie poured himself half a cup of coffee and added cream.

When they were settled back in their seats, Marcia gave them a friendly smile. "It is so nice to meet you. I notice here the reason for the visit, and I'm so sorry to learn of your son's death."

Marcia paused, and looked directly at Nora. "Please tell me about your son, Danny."

Charlie was surprised she moved to the subject of Danny so quickly, but Nora was ready to talk. "We lost our son in an accident recently, and instead of moving forward, our home is becoming more and more miserable." Tears came quickly, and she reached for a tissue on the table nearby.

"Our son was killed when his truck went through a barricade and crashed. Even now, I can hardly force myself to say the words."

Charlie took a sip from the Styrofoam coffee cup as Nora continued.

"My life is a nightmare, and it's affecting our marriage. Charlie works all day and doesn't get home until after 8 o'clock most nights. I am home alone all day with my thoughts. Friends invite me to get out of the house, but I have no desire to do anything or go anywhere. Most of the time, I can't even force myself to make supper." She looked down at her clenched fists resting in her lap, "Honestly, I don't see any reason to go on living."

Charlie shifted uncomfortably when Nora said she no longer wanted to live. He reached over and patted her arm and forced a smile.

"She does have her bad days, but, overall, she holds up pretty well."

Marcia turned her attention to Charlie. "How are *you* dealing with the death of your son?"

Something about the way she said *death of your son* pierced Charlie's heart. *Why is she focused on my feelings? I'm here to help Nora cope with losing Danny.* Without warning, his throat tightened and tears flooded his eyes. He swallowed down the sudden stab of grief and wondered if the counselor had noticed how well he controlled his emotions. When he described his feelings, his voice sounded artificial—fake--even to his own ears.

Halfway through the session Marcia turned the conversation to their backgrounds--especially, their parents.

Nora told about her devastation as a result of the sudden death of both parents in a plane crash five years earlier. She went into detail about the strong suspicion of a faulty landing gear and that lawyers were dealing with a class-action suit against the makers of the airplane.

"I know this may sound crazy, but, as bad as it was to deal with Mom and Dad's death, it isn't half as bad as what I'm going through now."

Marcia turned to Charlie. "Are your parents still living?"

"Yes, my daddy is the pastor of one of the largest Bible churches in the county."

The counselor scribbled a quick note on her pad. "What made him decide to become a pastor?"

"Well, my Daddy led a rough life when he was younger and got into some things he shouldn't have. But, as Daddy tells it, one night he heard the call on his life and he went forward in a revival meeting and prayed for God to forgive him."

Nora looked at Charlie, expecting him to tell the rest of the story--that JD had been drinking hard for two days and was in a drunken stupor when he went forward at that revival.

Marcia didn't seem quite satisfied with Charlie's answer. "What sort of trouble or rough life did your father have?"

"Well, he was known to get a little angry after he had a couple of drinks, and that sometimes got him into trouble."

"Did he ever drink to the point where he got drunk?"

"Oh, no. He would get a little agitated at us kids, but we probably deserved it." Charlie laughed nervously. "But, no, I don't think he ever got drunk."

Marcia stole a look at Nora as Charlie answered and noted her reaction.

"Were you allowed to talk or share your feelings in your home as a child?"

"Well, for the most part we were, but Daddy ruled the roost; no doubt about that. It was his way or the highway."

"Did you feel you were respected as a child and that your feelings were considered?"

Charlie's mind flashed back to being in trouble with his dad when he was a child, how JD took off his belt or picked up something with which to discipline him. And it wasn't just a couple of swats on his backside. No, he would grab him by the arm or even the hair and hold him with one hand while hitting him viciously with the belt. If Charlie screamed or begged, JD would tell him to shut up and stop crying or he would really give him something to cry about.

"Oh, sure. I felt respected as a child, and my parents always took my feeling into consideration."

Marcia unexpectedly changed her line of questioning. "What do you miss most about Danny?"

As Charlie tightened his grip on the Styrofoam cup, Marcia made another note on her pad.

Charlie wanted to tell her about the times Danny went to the shop with him on Saturday mornings and how they worked together when Danny helped him with a tune-up or even an engine overhaul. But when he opened his mouth, the words wouldn't come. His eyes filled with tears as he felt his face start to redden.

All at once, he was on his feet. "Where's the men's room?"

Marcia nodded toward the door. "Just off the waiting room."

Charlie excused himself and quickly found the men's room. Once safely inside, he locked the door and leaned against the tiled wall. He felt he might pass out. Slowly, he slid down the wall and sat on the floor. His heart was pounding and his pulse was racing.

He wondered if he was on the verge of a heart attack. Charlie wiped the beads of perspiration on his forehead on the sleeve of his shirt. Within a few moments he pulled himself together and stood.

He got up and turned on the cold water tap, cupping his hands under the faucet, and drinking from his hand. Then he splashed some water on his face. *I'll be okay. I just need to get out of here. This is harder than I thought it would be.*

By the time Charlie pulled himself together, the hour was up.

The traffic in Springfield was congested when they left the counselor's office, and for a while neither Charlie or Nora spoke. Once they got out of the heavy traffic and on the interstate, Nora turned her head to look at him.

"A penny for your thoughts. What did you think of her?"

"You can go back there if you want. I didn't get a single thing out of it. I could have spent that money on some new tools I've been needing for a long time."

Nora's tone was sharp. "I made another appointment for us, but if you aren't interested, I'll cancel it."

"I just don't see what good seeing her again will do. She seems to have a one-track mind about Danny and how much we miss him. Nothing she says is going to change how much we miss Danny, Nora, and neither is talking about our childhoods and our parents. Danny's gone, and nobody can do anything about it. We just need to learn to face the days ahead and feel happy again. But that gal seems interested in going backwards instead of forward. I'm just not interested in doing that."

They drove a few miles in silence, then Charlie looked at Nora out of the corner of his eye. "You probably noticed how bad it made me feel when she asked questions about him. That is why I had to leave and get out of there."

"Yes, I noticed," she said softly. "But..."

"But what?"

"Sometimes, Charlie, we have to look backwards so that we can see what is coming up behind us."

"What are you talking about?"

Nora didn't respond. However, she noticed how similar the words she had just spoken were printed on the rearview mirror.

When they got home, Nora went in the house and up the stairs while Charlie grabbed the mail on his way inside. There was an envelope from the firm that was handling the class action lawsuit involving Nora's parents. He pulled that envelope out and threw the junk mail on the kitchen table.

"Nora! There's something for you from the lawyers handling the lawsuit."

"Can you go ahead and open it for me?"

He was scanning the letter when Nora came down the stairs.

"This is very interesting," he said, as he handed her the letter.

Nora had consented, along with the other survivors to allow the law firm to represent them. The class action suit was against the makers of the plane and the manufacturers of the landing gear. After many months of investigation and fact-finding, the Federal Aviation Association felt there had been negligence from the company that engineered and manufactured the landing gear.

This letter informed them that there would be an important meeting held in Springfield in two weeks and that everyone involved in the suit should attend. It went on to say that the case would likely go to trial, but that there were important decisions to be made as the lawyers prepared to move forward.

CHAPTER TWENTY-SEVEN

S andy sat in the office of her cheerleading coach, Heidi. The coach had asked to meet with Sandy so they could talk. Heidi, wearing purple and gray sweats--her usual attire--sat behind her desk across from Sandy.

"Sandy, I asked you to come talk to me because the other girls on the squad are concerned about you. I wanted to visit with you to see if I can help. Can you share with me how you're doing since..."

"Since Danny died? I loved him; we had talked about getting married after we graduated."

"I knew you two were serious, but I didn't know you were engaged."

"We weren't officially engaged. We never told anyone, but that's what we were planning. I even showed him a picture of the kind of wedding gown I wanted."

"I'm so sorry for what's happened, Sandy. Danny's death has been a blow to the whole student body, and I've noticed it's hard for you to put on a happy face and lead the others in the cheers, and believe me, you have my deepest sympathy. But it's my responsibility to do what's best for the squad and to make sure our school is represented in the best possible light. I need you to step up. You're head cheerleader, and it's important that you lead the other girls by example. They count on you for that, and I'm counting on you too. I know you don't realize it right now, but you have your whole life ahead of you, and I'm asking you to get back into the swing of things. I know you can't do it overnight, but within the next couple of weeks, I'm going to need to see the old Sandy heading up the squad, or I'll have to ask you to take some time off."

The next morning, Sandy left a note on Heidi's desk. It was a note of resignation announcing that she was not only resigning from her cheerleading position, she was dropping out of school.

Sandy cleaned out her locker, and then lingered a while next to Danny's empty locker. She closed her eyes, softly kissed the metal door and ran her hand across it. Then she turned and walked down the long hallway and out the door for the last time.

On her way home, Sandy stopped by the Boar's Head to see her friend, Maria. The two girls had known each other for two years—since Sandy had started working there part time.

Since Danny's death, Maria was the one person who seemed to understand what Sandy was going through. Sandy felt safe with Maria, and she often stopped by the Boar's Head when she knew Maria was there.

Maria was refilling the salt and pepper shakers that were assembled on a large brown tray. Business was slow and no one else was around when Sandy arrived to tell her about the conversation with Heidi.

"I can't believe it! You can't just turn off your feelings like that. You need time to get over what happened!"

"I can't really blame her. Since Danny died, I can't concentrate in class, I don't even try to do my homework. To tell you the truth, I just don't care about anything anymore. The other cheerleaders are mad at me and some of them don't even talk to me because they say I make them sad. I just can't take it anymore."

"So, what are you going to do?"

"I don't know, but I've been thinking about going away, just getting out of this town. Maybe I will go to St. Louis and stay with my Aunt Olga for a while. She is my favorite aunt and she lives alone. I'm pretty sure she would let me stay with her; she has an extra bedroom. I could get a job there and get my GED. It's just that there are so many memories of Danny here, I feel like I can't stand it."

"It sounds like you've made up your mind and you're really going to do this."

"Yeah, I'm going to tell my parents. They aren't going to like it, and they'll try to talk me out of it, but I'm pretty stubborn. I've got to get away from here."

By noon that day, the faculty and the student body at the high school knew that Sandy was leaving. The next morning, Charlie was having breakfast at the Boar's Head.

"She's doing what?"

"Yeah, she told me yesterday."

"But why?"

"The memories. It's the memories, Charlie. I think it's just too much for her. She said she can't sleep, she can't concentrate at school. The poor thing barely eats, and she spends most of her free time out at the cemetery. She even went out there and tried to do her homework."

"I've been so focused on Nora I haven't given as much thought to Sandy as I should have."

Charlie finished up his breakfast, paid his bill at the cash register, and walked across the street to work. But he couldn't get the thought of Sandy leaving town out of his mind.

Nora was in bad shape too, much worse than Sandy, and she didn't seem to be getting any better. She had no interest in the house, cooking, or even taking care of herself.

He was preoccupied all day by thoughts of what, if anything, he could do to help Nora.

Nora was on the couch, still in her robe when Charlie got home after work.

"Any mail today?"

Nora nodded toward the kitchen table where an assortment of junk mail was scattered. Charlie glanced through it.

Nora called to him. "There is something on the table I had to sign for....a registered letter."

Charlie spotted it, unopened. It was from the law firm that was handling the class action lawsuit.

The letter was an announcement of an out-of-court settlement that resulted in each of the plaintiffs receiving seven hundred and fifty thousand dollars.

Charlie suddenly whistled and whooped so loudly that it startled her. "Nora, listen to this!"

She raised up on one arm as he rushed into the room and began reading the letter out loud.

"Three quarters of a million dollars, baby!" He grabbed Nora, hugging her so tightly she nearly lost her breath, "Baby, do you know what this means? Now we can do what we really want to do. We are free."

"What do you mean?" she asked.

"We don't have to stay in this town if we don't want to....we are free to do whatever we want."

Nora nodded and tried to understand what Charlie was getting at. She would find out soon enough.

CHAPTER TWENTY-EIGHT

Charlie kept calling the settlement their key to freedom. "We could get a new house, or travel. This settlement will allow us to take our lives in any direction we want."

Nora was trying to garner enough enthusiasm so that Charlie wouldn't notice her lack of excitement.

"But, you know what I really think we should do with this money? Charlie asked.

"No, what?"

"I know Daddy and Mother won't like it, but I would really love to move away from Ladner and find another place where there aren't so many sad memories. You don't know all the painful memories I deal with, day in and day out."

Charlie was right, she didn't know about his pain because he didn't usually share his feelings with her. "What sort of memories are you talking about?"

Charlie's face darkened. "Every day, when I go to work, I think about his truck. Then, every time I road test a car, I pull up short of going on down to Devil's Elbow like I used to do. Every time I look at my tool box, I see the tools Danny used to call his own; the ones down on the lower shelf. When I see those tools of his...."

She covered his hand with hers.

"Nora, we both know this town is loaded with painful memories of Danny. I just think it would be best for us if we got away from it all--started a new life somewhere else."

For the first time, Nora got a small glimpse of the pain Charlie had concealed. She began to think of what it would be like to get away from the place where Danny had lived....and died.

They decided they wouldn't tell anyone about the money. There wouldn't be a press release announcing the settlement for a couple weeks, according to the letter they received. That would give them time to think and decide for sure what they wanted to do.

Over the next few days, Nora thought about her parents more than she had for a long time. Then, one evening, she shared some of her thoughts with Charlie.

"You know, Mom and Dad always gave so much of themselves to helping others. They taught me the way to true happiness is in helping those who are less fortunate. Whatever we decide to do, I would like to find a way to help other people."

"Are you suggesting we just give it all away to the poor?"

"No, no, I don't mean that, although we might give some of it away. I'm just thinking out loud. But I would like to do something that would honor the way my parents lived."

Soon, it was decided they would try to find a way to fulfill Charlie's desire to get out of Ladner and Nora's wishes to honor the memory of her parents. The solution came the very next Sunday just after the morning church service.

Charlie was scanning the bulletin board as he waited in the foyer of the church. He was scanning the various messages as Nora finished a conversation with Anna. He noticed an appeal for volunteer help at a summer camp in North Carolina. The organizers of the camp announced they were devoting the entire summer program to helping single-parent families, and they were looking for willing volunteers to serve food and help with a program for the children. But what really caught Charlie's attention was their need for someone with mechanical experience. The camp director needed someone to service the cars and make other repairs too.

Charlie took out his pen and scribbled the contact information on his church bulletin. When Nora joined him and they walked toward their car, Charlie glanced toward Danny's grave. He was beginning to have second thoughts about leaving Ladner.

They stopped for a quick lunch, and as Charlie ate and Nora picked at her food, he told her what he had found on the bulletin board at the church. Nora was interested.

After they finished lunch and back in the car, Charlie admitted there was something bothering him. "You know, now that we have found something that seems like it would work for us, I'm thinking twice about taking off and leaving Danny here in Ladner."

Nora's eyes filled with tears. "I thought about that, too. I don't know who would take care of his grave and decorate it on Memorial Day and put out flowers on his birthday. It won't be easy to leave him behind."

Charlie was conflicted. He had a strong desire to get out of Ladner, but he still felt responsible for taking care of his son.

The following day Charlie was taking a test drive and decided to pull into the cemetery for just a few moments. As he approached Danny's grave, he noticed a man on his hands and knees over a grave stone. Charlie thought he recognized the person kneeling, and, sure enough, it was Micah. After the fiasco at Danny's funeral, all had been forgiven and Micah continued to work at the church. However, Charlie was surprised to see him in the cemetery.

Charlie stopped the car, got out, and walked toward Micah. It looked as though Micah had been praying or meditating.

"Micah? What are you doing here? I didn't know you knew anyone in here."

Surprised to see Charlie, he responded, "I don't talk much about it, but this is the place where my wife and...." His eyes turned to the smallest headstone near the one that obviously belonged to his wife. Little angels were inscribed in the pink granite. The two men stood in silence for a few minutes and Charlie began to gain understanding into the sad look Micah carried most of the time.

"I didn't know."

"Yeah, for the longest time I thought it might just go away if I didn't mention it. My parents and grandparents are buried here, too. For many years, I stayed away from here—from anything that reminded me." He rested his hand on the larger of the two markers."

"But now, I try to come here as often as I can. I guess it's the reason I took the job here at the church—to be close to my family. I've learned a lot from my AA friends.".

Charlie looked at Micah in a different light.

"Micah, there aren't many people who know this, but Nora and I are thinking about leaving Ladner. It might be temporary, or it might be permanent; we just aren't sure yet. But if we go, we will need someone to look after Danny's grave. I was just wondering--"

"Sure, Charlie, I would be honored to take care of Danny's grave for you and Nora."

Charlie smiled, and the two men shook hands on the agreement they had just made.

Charlie started to walk back to the car, but turned back with one more request. "Please don't mention this to anyone. I haven't told my dad yet, but when I do, I'm sure he will make an announcement in church. So, please keep this to yourself until I tell him."

Micah nodded, then watched Charlie walk away, the gravel crunching beneath his shoes.

As Charlie drove away, he looked over his shoulder toward his dad's office window and wondered if his dad had seen him at the cemetery. Charlie knew he would not be pleased.

CHAPTER TWENTY-NINE

J D and Anna were just finishing lunch and still sitting at the kitchen table when Charlie walked through the front door without knocking.

"Well, come in, son; we're so glad you came by." JD gestured toward one of the empty chairs.

Charlie sat down and scooted up to the table. His mother offered to get him a piece of blueberry cobbler and a cup of coffee. As she warmed it up and added a scoop of vanilla ice cream, they made small talk about the weather and things going on with some of the church members.

Finally, Charlie took a deep breath and dived in to the reason he was there.

"Dad, Mom, I know you're aware of what it's been like for me and Nora since Danny died."

They nodded in unison.

"Everywhere we turn, there are reminders of Danny."

"For us, too," JD added.

"But, Daddy, I feel like I can't stand it any longer. Sometimes I think I'm going to lose my mind. Just last Saturday, I was working under the hood of a car and I looked up and thought I saw Danny standing over by the parts washer, cleaning parts for me, just like he used to."

The coffee cup trembled in Charlie's hand. "Every time I go to work I think about his truck and try to figure out what happened that night. I can't take a test drive out toward Devil's Elbow or drive by the high school. No matter what I do, something or someone triggers that pain."

Charlie put his cup on the table and looked at his dad and then his mother.

"The worst thing, though, is being at home. I can't go into his room or even open the door, but Nora spends half her time in there, because she says she feels close to him there. When I see Spike in the back yard with the Frisbee in his mouth like he's waiting for Danny to come outside, I feel like I can't breathe, it hurts so much. I feel like I have to get away from Ladner."

JD took a deep breath and started to speak, but Charlie didn't notice and kept on talking.

"Sunday, I saw a special notice on the bulletin board at church. There's a summer camp near Asheville, North Carolina, and they're looking for someone with mechanic skills to work on the cars and help single parents learn how to take care of their own vehicles. Most of the campers are women who have never worked on anything that required a wrench, and they need to learn how to do these things."

"Wait a minute, son," JD interrupted. "That sounds like a worthwhile thing to do, but you have a job, and you can't just walk away from making a living to go volunteer in North Carolina."

"But that's just it, Daddy. Nora is getting a 750,000-dollar settlement from her folks' accident. That's what is making this possible for us."

JD's eyebrows lifted as he calculated ten percent of that amount of money.

Charlie had not thought much about tithing on the settlement, but as he saw his dad's excited and pleased reaction to the dollar amount, he knew exactly what JD was thinking.

"They are advertising for mechanics to go live there and work on the cars. The people who will be coming to the camp live barely above the poverty line."

Charlie stopped talking a moment to give his parents a chance to digest all he had told them.

"I can do this! I can take my tools and some of the things we need and we can go live there for a while."

JD was in complete agreement. "Son, I understand what you're saying. No doubt you're hurting because of all the reminders of Danny around Ladner." He looked across the table at Anna.

"Your mother and I will not stand in your way. If God is in this, it will work out for the two of you." JD scooted his chair back from the table and raised his hand as though giving his blessing. "This settlement is a sign to me that God has his hand on you. You should follow this special leading from the Lord."

JD leaned forward. "You know, son, I really believe God has smiled on you with this large sum of money. God knows of your and Nora's faithfulness across the years here in our church."

JD grinned and almost winked as if they were co-conspirators. "I know what people put in the offering plate every Sunday, so I know that you and Nora are faithful to God with your tithe."

Charlie braced for the "paid up and prayed up" speech and felt anger stirring in his heart. If God protects the families of those who are faithful givers, where was Danny's guardian angel when he approached Devil's Elbow that foggy night?

Charlie decided there was nothing to be gained by hurling that question at his dad, so he kept his thoughts to himself. If everything went as he hoped, he and Nora would soon be leaving town.

When Charlie left, he felt he had his parents' support, and he was grateful JD had not asked him to reimburse them for the expense of Danny's funeral.

Charlie called a realtor and made an appointment. Later, that same day, he placed a letter of application to the camp in North Carolina advising them of his availability to spend the summer there working as a mechanic. He hoped leaving Ladner would be the end of painful memories. He couldn't get out of Ladner fast enough.

CHAPTER THIRTY

The bright red For Sale sign was planted in the front lawn the following Monday. Once the sign was in place, Nora began having second thoughts, but she had already agreed with Charlie about making the change. So, she started the hard work of preparing for the move.

Anna promised to help her pack, so the two of them tackled the job, one closet and one room at a time.

The process was orderly and organized as the two women worked together. But Nora told Anna explicitly that she would pack Danny's room herself--by herself.

When the time came to face that task, Anna put her arm around Nora and asked again, "Are you sure you want to do this alone?"

"Yes," Nora said. "I need to do this. I hope you understand."

Nora had put it off as long as she could. She even worked with Charlie in the garage, trying to help him with the monumental task of deciding what to get rid of and what to keep.

When it could no longer be avoided, she opened the door to Danny's room and dragged in two large storage containers. No one had been in Danny's room since his death except her, and she hadn't moved a thing since the day she picked out his funeral clothes. She placed the containers on the floor in the middle of the room and looked around slowly. *What should I keep; what should I part with?*

The blue quilt was a keepsake she couldn't possibly part with. Danny loved the posters of cars and motorcycles on the wall, and they wouldn't take up much room. Danny had found the bedside lamp at a garage sale when he was about ten years old, and she knew she could find a place for it.

Nora sat on the edge of the bed to gather her thoughts. Everything in the room was a piece of her son's life. She was confronted with the notion that she could not throw any of these precious items away. It would be like throwing away pieces of Danny's life. She could not possibly do that yet; she would wait until some other time to make these heavy decisions. She lovingly packed every item.

She dragged in more storage containers, and when she was finished, there were six large ones stacked in his room. She secured each lid, then she tore off a ten inch section of masking tape and secured it to the top. With a felt-tipped pen, she marked each container with Danny's name.

Charlie, too, was running into memories in the basement and the garage. Danny's bike, ball caps, bats, ball gloves, and even his baseball cleats were all kept in one corner of the garage. Charlie planned to keep Danny's favorite bat and perhaps one of his son's favorite hats. He was going to sell the bike. However, in the end, he couldn't leave anything behind.

Charlie decided to ask his mom and dad if they had room to store some of Danny's things. He was certain there was room either in his dad's garage or in the storage shed behind the house.

Even after several showings by their real estate agent, Charlie and Nora had no offers on the house. However, one family wanted to lease it for a year. It seemed to be the best way to go. Papers were signed and the deal was made.

The church held a farewell party for them before they left for North Carolina. Charlie rented the largest U-Haul trailer he could find, and it was packed solid with everything they felt necessary for their trip. He had debated with Nora about the number of containers marked with Danny's name, but Nora would not budge. Every container held a piece of their son, and she would not part with any of them. In the end, JD and Anna stored more items than they had originally agreed upon.

JD wanted he, Anna, Nora, and Charlie to have prayer together before his son and daughter-in-law left Ladner. He had not seen the hoped-for check in the treasurer's report and thought a strong prayer might serve as a useful reminder for Charlie to "pay up" before leaving.

As the four of them stood in a tight circle, holding hands, JD cleared his throat and began. In his most authoritative preacher's voice, he prayed. *Our precious Heavenly Father, we come to you this day and ask for your protection upon our family. We ask that you cover our son and daughter-in-law with your hand as they embark on this journey.* JD's voice grew louder. *Only you know how dangerous the highways can be this time of year and how many drunk drivers there are on these roadways. We know you are the master of the universe and you have your protective hand upon those who love you and who are obedient, yes, obedient to you".*

The emphasis was not lost on Charlie. But this was one time Charlie wasn't going to be bullied by JD. As they finished the prayer and prepared to leave, Charlie and Nora hugged the older couple. Tears were streaming down the cheeks of both women, but father and son did what the Davis men always did; they simply shook hands and said goodbye.

Charlie and Nora made one last stop on their way out of town. It was hard to maneuver the trailer on the narrow gravel roads of the cemetery, but within minutes they were at Danny's graveside.

Nora was the first one out of the car. The sky was overcast and they could barely hear the raindrops falling softly on the gravel. Charlie looked for an umbrella, but it had already been packed. He found a piece of cardboard in the back seat and took it where Nora stood and held it over her head as she reached down and lovingly touched Danny's headstone.

CHAPTER THIRTY-ONE

I t was nearly 750 miles from Ladner to Asheville, North Carolina. Pulling the trailer behind them, Charlie figured it would take two days, maybe more, to get there. They stopped for the night in Nashville and made it to the campground near Asheville late on the second day. Neither of them mentioned Danny during the long drive.

The first thing they saw when they drove through the gated entrance of the retreat center was the huge granite sign on the side of the hill. Ridgeview Camp. The letters were chiseled into the side of the boulder. They could see for several miles across the beautiful Smoky Mountains. The view was breath-taking.

Nora waited in the car with the windows down, admiring the streaming yellow and orange colors of the Carolina sunset while Charlie was inside getting the keys to their new home.

Nora deeply inhaled the pristine, pure air, and closed her eyes and prayed this would be a new beginning for the two of them. She was beginning to feel excited--even eager--to set up a new home as they began this new chapter.

Within minutes, Charlie was back with the keys and an information packet in hand. He stood outside the car with a map, trying to orient himself to the direction he should take. The camp was larger than he imagined. Nora leaned over and spoke through the open window excitedly, "Well, where is it, and what did they say?"

Charlie pointed as he explained, "It's a two bedroom cabin. I think it is just down that way, around the corner and beyond that grove of trees behind the camp tabernacle." Charlie slid behind the wheel and started the car as he continued. "Behind the camp chapel is the maintenance barn and next to it is the place where we will stay."

Nora heard the excitement in Charlie's voice.

"I think this place will be really convenient for me. It won't take me long to walk over to the shop. Look at those hills, Nora. We are going to love this."

Charlie handed the keys and information packet to Nora as he drove toward their cabin.

As he eased the car and trailer toward their new place, he noticed how narrow the roads were, and he was reminded of the one-lane roads in the cemetery in Ladner. There was a quick stab of pain, but it didn't last long.

As they made the turn behind the camp chapel, they saw the maintenance garage—or the barn, as some called it.

Charlie and Nora's cottage was just a stone's throw from the barn. Nora loved it at first sight. Pink impatiens bloomed in the shade near the front steps. Made of logs, it appeared the building materials came from the lumber harvested in the wooded area surrounding the camp. There was an inviting glider on the front porch, and Nora pictured herself sitting there with Charlie in the cool of the evening, listening to the sounds of nature.

Charlie backed the trailer as close to the door as he could. They got out of the car and stood there a moment sizing up the place. The sun was nearly over the horizon, but they could see enough to know they loved it.

Their cottage was modest and plain, with about twenty feet of sidewalk leading to the porch. When Charlie turned the key in the door and they walked inside, they were surprised to see that it was furnished with all the necessary appliances. There were two chairs, a loveseat, a small drop-leaf table, and even a small fireplace. On the table was a bouquet of yellow roses with an envelope attached.

Nora went to the table and picked up the small envelope. She wondered who could have known that yellow roses were her favorites. She opened the note: *Welcome to your new home. Love & prayers, JD & Anna.* Just under their names was a scripture reference, Malachi 3:10.

Nora leaned over and smelled one of the roses as she spoke. "It was sweet of them to remember us, Charlie. Look at these beautiful roses! Do you know what Malachi 3:10 says?"

The flowers' fragrance reminded Charlie of the front of the sanctuary at Danny's funeral. He knew what the scripture said. "Bring the whole tithe into the storehouse." He seethed quietly but said nothing. He decided to let Nora think his folks were sending flowers out of the goodness of their hearts.

They were still getting acquainted with the place when there was a soft knock at the door, and when Charlie opened it he was surprised to see about a dozen other volunteers. They had come to help unload the trailer. They all pitched in, and within 45 minutes every box was in the cottage. The women wanted to help Nora unpack, but she put them off, saying she would handle the rest of it alone.

Someone appeared with three gallons of ice cream and several toppings to enjoy as they all stayed and visited. Charlie and

Nora were thrilled with this new beginning; it seemed far from Ladner--and very different.

Early the next morning, Charlie pulled back the curtain to see if he could catch a glimpse of the North Carolina sunrise, something he had heard others rave about. Looking through the window, all he saw was a dense, gray fog. He flinched as dark memories consumed him, and he quickly let the curtain drop back into place.

Turning to Nora, he asked, "What are we going to do for breakfast?" The words were barely out of his mouth when there was a knock on the door. Charlie pulled on his jeans and slipped a T shirt over his head before he crossed the living room barefoot to the front door.

On the other side was a little lady holding a beautiful breakfast tray complete with a simple bouquet of daisies in a small, blue vase. There was hot coffee in a carafe, and he got a whiff of warm cinnamon and sugar from the just-baked rolls. There was also a bowl of fresh strawberries and slices of cantaloupe.

Millie knew the new couple was coming, but she hadn't been able to help move them in the night before, so she welcomed them to Ridgeview with a breakfast tray.

Charlie figured her to be at least 65 years old and surmised she was probably a long-time volunteer at the camp. Her face was kind, and her hair was cut short and nearly all gray. He liked her immediately. She was wearing jeans and a sweatshirt with a washed-out Ridgeview logo on the front.

She thrust the tray into Charlie's hands, "We have been expecting you. Glad to see you made it here in one piece. Ralph, my husband, is the one you will be working with in the shop."

Nora had slipped her robe on and came up behind Charlie. She quickly maneuvered around him, took the tray, and set it on the drop-leaf table. Sticking out her hand, Nora smiled and spoke cheerfully, "Hi, I'm Nora, and we are so glad to finally be here. Thank you for going to the trouble of bringing breakfast to us.

Charlie had just wondered what we were going to do about break-fast when we heard your knock."

Millie beamed at Nora as if she was a long-lost friend. "I wanted you to know that we have been looking forward to having you here with us. Ralph will be down to meet you soon."

Millie pointed through the open door toward her cabin as she spoke, "Ours is the one just up the way. When the fog clears, you will be able to see it. It's only fifty yards away."

CHAPTER THIRTY-TWO

It was the in-between time for the staff. Charlie and Nora arrived on a Friday evening, and most of the camp programs ran Monday through Friday. The campers from the most recent session had packed up and said their goodbyes, and the staff was gearing down to catch their breath before the next group arrived Monday morning.

There were 25 full-time, adult volunteers, besides those who came in from the nearby towns to work part time. The volunteers did just about everything from preparing food in the camp kitchen to brushing down the horses in the corral.

Whatever needed to be done, a volunteer did it. If the camp director thought more flowers should be planted by the sign near the entrance, a volunteer did it. If the concrete floor in the chapel needed to be swept, a volunteer took care of it.

Many of the adult volunteers were like Charlie and Nora and had taken an early retirement to volunteer at the Bible camp. Most of them were motivated by a desire to be a positive example of the love of Jesus to the children. Many of them had grown children who had strayed from the faith and saw this as a second chance to point a young boy or girl in the right direction.

Charlie and Nora expected the subject of family and children to come up when they arrived at the camp. Charlie wanted to pretend they were childless. He felt if the other volunteers and campers knew they were grieving, it might make things awkward. At first, Nora disagreed, but in the end, she decided to go along with Charlie's wishes to keep it a secret. She, too, noticed that people became uncomfortable when Danny's death came up in a conversation. If the other staff and campers didn't know, she would not have to face their pity. It was against her better judgment to not talk about their son. She would try to go along with the idea but she knew it would be hard.

After Millie excused herself, promising she would be back in an hour to help Nora unpack the boxes, Charlie and Nora sat at the table and enjoyed breakfast. The cinnamon rolls were wonderful, and Charlie thought the coffee nearly as good as it was at the Boar's Head.

"I'm going to miss my buddies at the Boar's Head," he said, then changed the subject. "How long do you think it's going to take to unpack these boxes?"

Nora turned and sized up the boxes. Then she looked at the large plastic containers that had Danny's name in large letters on them.

"Charlie, are you sure it's a good idea to keep Danny's death a secret?" She nodded toward the stack. For the second time since he awakened, he flinched.

"We already talked about this. I think we should just keep quiet about it. I have some tape in the car. I'll take care of it."

Putting down his coffee mug, he went outside and quickly returned with the tape. With one quick yank on the end of the roll, he easily tore off a piece and stuck it over his son's name. He did the same with the other containers that had Danny's name on them.

An hour later, Millie, true to her word, came down the narrow road with Ralph close behind. Ralph was a soft-spoken guy, and it became clear right away that he always deferred to Millie. She was the talker while he enjoyed staying back.

Ralph had an easy and relaxed way about him that people liked. His eyes had a blue-green tint that, coupled with his full beard, made him seem knowledgeable and wise. Like Millie, he wore jeans, but his fingernails bore the telltale stubborn oil stains that were the trademark of most mechanics. Ralph wore a long-sleeved sweatshirt to guard against the cool Carolina morning.

Charlie immediately noticed the logo on Ralph's cap—the University of Missouri Tigers. Danny had worn an identical hat. Charlie had a hard time taking his eyes off Ralph's hat, but he put out his hand.

"Hi, I'm Charlie Davis, and this is my wife, Nora." Ralph reached out to shake hands and Charlie recognized the calloused hand of a fellow mechanic.

Ralph gave a shy grin and responded, "Name here is Ralph, and we've been looking forward to meeting you. We've heard about your mechanic skills, and we can sure use you here."

Ralph pointed toward the barn. "I can get by with what I know, but we need someone who *really* knows his stuff."

While the women started unpacking the boxes in the kitchen, Ralph and Charlie walked over to the shop where Ralph kept a small wagon that he thought they could use to move the heavy boxes that contained Charlie's tools.

Taking the keys from his pocket and opening the door to the shop, Ralph explained, "This building used to be the chapel. When we outgrew it, the new one was built. They didn't know what to do with this building, but someone suggested we turn it into the maintenance garage, and it's worked out real well. You can't see it from the highway, so we're sort of hidden back here in the trees.

We use it for the repair shop during the camping season, and when the camp is closed down, we use it for storing equipment."

As soon as the door opened, Charlie sniffed the familiar scent of gasoline and oil. The old building had a lofty ceiling, which was about fifteen feet at its highest point—like a cathedral.

The length of the shop was just short of sixty-five feet, and at the far end, near the top, was a wooden cross that some of the campers had put together during a retreat. Charlie quickly judged the cross to be about ten feet long, and there were dust-covered pictures on either side of it that measured four feet by eight feet each. One picture depicted Jesus holding a little lamb in one arm and a staff in the other. The picture on the opposite side of the cross was of Jesus standing at the door of the Palestinian home, knocking. JD carried the same wallet-size picture with him and used it when he was doing personal evangelism so sinners could see how Jesus is trying to come into their hearts.

Ralph laughed and nodded toward the cross, "I'll bet you never worked in a shop like this. When they built the new chapel five years ago, they didn't want this worn out cross and the pictures, so they just left 'em up on the wall. I don't mind 'em, though, because it reminds me that my work as a mechanic is just as important as what the preachers do next door."

After a quick look around, Ralph helped Charlie bring in his tools and arrange them neatly near a workbench. Charlie felt right at home.

Nora and Millie were hard at work making the cottage comfortable and homey. Many of the boxes had been emptied, but the containers holding Danny's things were still in the middle of the room, unopened.

Nora had taken some things to the bedroom to put away, and when she returned to the living room, Millie had opened one of Danny's containers and had pulled out his letter jacket.

"Ralph told me he barely missed getting one of these when he was a kid." She held the jacket up admiringly. "What position did Charlie play?"

"I think he was the quarterback."

"What does this star here mean? Was he a star?"

"Well, he...he...yes, he was a star. He was captain of the team."

Nora took the jacket from Millie. "I'll just put this in the closet, and then let's take a break. Does that sound like a good idea to you?" Nora felt sick--like she had betrayed Danny by denying he ever existed. *I can't do this. Charlie and I are going to have another talk.*

CHAPTER THIRTY-THREE

At twelve noon, the large bell by the cafeteria signaled it was time to eat. It was a clear, clarion ring that could be heard throughout the camp.

Although workers sometimes had lunch in their own cabins, most of the time they ate together in their own dining space, which was a small area just off the main dining room from where the campers had their meals. The staff could keep an eye on the kids, but they were able to enjoy socializing while the kids had lunch. And it was much quieter.

Ralph and Charlie walked out of the shop just as their wives stepped onto the porch of the cottage.

"My stomach is telling me it's about lunch time," Millie called out. "Ralph, let's walk up to the cafeteria and introduce Nora and Charlie to the others."

The cafeteria was located uphill from the cottages. It was a five-minute walk up the asphalt trail, but some staff used the golf carts when they were available.

Charlie and Nora were winded when they reached the cafeteria, but Ralph and Millie were accustomed to the rigorous walk.

Before they went inside, Charlie had to stop and catch his breath. He bent over, hands on his thighs. "Man, I didn't realize I was so out of shape."

As he was bent over, breathing deeply, he noticed the small cast-iron plaque affixed to the bottom of the frame that held the huge dinner bell. "In memory of our son, Bobby Addison, 1942-1957. May he be remembered every time this bell rings."

Charlie quickly looked away. His chest felt uneasy and his heart seemed to skip a few beats. He felt light-headed and quickly sat down on the step, pretending to tie his shoelace. The others stood looking out over the vista as Millie pointed out the various features of the camp. As Charlie sat there, pulling himself together, he wondered when the pain of Danny's death would lessen. After a two-day drive, he still hadn't outrun it.

Charlie and Nora were introduced to nine people before they got in line to pick up their plates. Ralph simply introduced Charlie as the new mechanic from Missouri, the Show-Me State! Millie introduced Nora as her new friend and explained it hadn't been decided what her job would be. Everyone understood exactly what that meant; it was important to be flexible and willing to do whatever needed to be done.

When the campers were finishing eating, Joe Wright, the camp director, asked for everyone's attention and stood at the front of the room.

"It's great to see you all here today, and I hope you have been able to rest up from last week. Before I talk about the campers who will be here next week, let me introduce you to our new workers who just arrived last night; Charlie and Nora Davis. They drove all the way from Ladner, Missouri." Joe motioned to them, "Charlie and Nora, stand up so everyone can see you."

Charlie and Nora scooted back from the table and stood half-way as the others clapped.

"Charlie will be working down in the shop with Ralph. I have been told Charlie can fix anything from a tricycle to a dump truck." There was more clapping and laughter.

Joe looked straight at Charlie as he continued, "You arrived just in time. We have two pick-up trucks we depend on that I'm confident you can fix. This is another example of how God has been providing for us!"

Joe hesitated a moment, and Millie spoke up. "Yes, and he was quarterback and captain of the football team back in his day."

Charlie shot a shocked look at Nora, wondering where Millie had come up with that false story. Charlie's high school football career had ended with an injury during his sophomore year. Nora didn't meet his eyes. *Oh, what a tangled web.*

Joe thanked the volunteers for making the previous camping week a success and gave a rundown of the campers who would be attending the coming week. He had everyone's attention.

"Tomorrow afternoon, we expect nearly 250 adults and kids to arrive." Joe looked down at his clipboard. "The kids range from four years of age to sixteen. The adults are, for the most part, women who are coming from the Charlotte and Asheville areas. Most of them live at or below the poverty level."

Gesturing to Charlie and Ralph, Joe directed his words straight at the mechanics. "You guys are going to have your hands full. We always try to do some brake jobs, oil changes, and maybe some simple tune-ups while they are here. So, if you two need some of us to come down to the shop and pitch in, just let me know."

Ralph nudged Charlie and whispered, "I hope you're ready for this!"

Joe went on. "This week is going to be more intense than last week, so get some good rest tonight. Tomorrow we have something special for you. Our camp speaker is coming early to spend time with us prior to the arrival of the campers. We will assemble in the chapel at 10 o'clock for a worship service. I know you will be blessed by the preaching of Brother Eddie Sutton. Eddie has worked with single adults at one of our largest churches in Charlotte, and he has a good understanding of the ways we can best relate to them."

After the noon meal, Charlie and Ralph spent the afternoon organizing their work stations, while Nora and Millie stayed busy organizing and tidying the cottage.

The men were amazed by the cottage's transformation into an inviting and comfortable home by the end of the day. Millie had managed to slip off to her own kitchen and the fresh-baked aroma of her chocolate chip cookies welcomed them.

Charlie froze when he spotted Danny's picture on the fireplace mantle. He made a quick recovery, hoping Nora had not gone back on her word. Neither Ralph nor Millie asked about the picture or even seemed to notice it, but Charlie was irritated at Nora for placing it there.

CHAPTER THIRTY-FOUR

The next day at 10:00 a.m. sharp, the camp workers gathered at the front of the chapel for the Sunday service. Its layout was much like the barn, but this chapel was newer and larger with a seating capacity of 500. The benches were rough-hewn oak, built by a group of retired carpenters from Asheville. Adults found them hard to sit on for even an hour, but the children didn't mind at all. The floors were concrete and required daily sweeping.

There was a piano and an organ down front, and the pulpit sat in the middle with a microphone attached. Along both side-walls were oversized windows that were kept open in the summer. A huge exhaust fan was high up in the back, and drew in a fresh breeze when it became hot. On the front wall and behind the pulpit was a large stained glass window that was almost identical to the one in JD's church in Ladner.

Charlie and Nora noticed it immediately. "It's going to be hard to sit in here and not think about Danny's funeral," Charlie said softly to Nora.

They took their seats and waited for the meeting to start. Charlie closed his eyes and thought about his buddies at the Boar's Head to keep him from thinking about Danny.

Millie was the camp pianist, and she accompanied the song leader as she led the volunteers in a few tunes they all knew by heart.

After the singing, Joe introduced Eddie Sutton. "Let's give him a hand as he comes to prepare us for the storm of campers that will hit tomorrow!"

At Eddie's request, the workers were all assembled on the benches on the right side of the chapel so he wouldn't need to speak into a microphone from the pulpit. He stood in front and close to the volunteers.

Eddie wore faded blue jeans and a sky blue cotton shirt that highlighted his blue eyes. His long hair was tied back in a ponytail.

Charlie sized him up immediately as the type of guy that he and his buddies often discussed at the Boar's Head—the long-haired, grungy types with loose morals that were responsible for the American decline. JD often spoke badly of such men in his sermons. It was one of JD's judgments that Charlie actually agreed with.

"Thank you, Joe, for your kind introduction and for allowing me to speak here today." He walked slowly back and forth in front of the group. "I don't know what your expectations are as far as the families, especially the kids, who will be arriving here tomorrow." He had the full attention of the volunteers.

"For the most part, we will have a lot of moms here with their kids. Many of the women are divorced; some are widows. "I hope you will be especially aware of the children and that you will be prepared for what you might be facing as you work with them. A lot of these kids have been traumatized by their parents' divorce. In addition, there will be several children here who are grieving the death of their fathers and women mourning the death of their husbands."

One of the volunteers raised his hand. "Didn't you mean to include single dads too?"

Eddie smiled and shook his head. "I looked over the camp registration and there are no dads accompanying children this week. In my experience, this is not unusual. Men generally cannot or will not bring their families to something like this because they feel they can handle it on their own. They tend to stay away from talking to others about the pain and challenges of being a single parent."

Charlie shifted uneasily in his seat.

"When it comes to the pain of grief and loss, women are usually the ones who mourn their losses, while men tend to replace their loss with something else."

Nora glanced sideways at Charlie.

"Adults usually know how to deal with grief and pain, but children don't have the words for it. This is one reason why we have camp experiences like this."

Eddie continued to walk back and forth across the front. "When the kids start to act up and cause trouble, maybe even get in fights, I hope you will remember the words of Jesus when he gathered the precious children around and said to his disciples, 'Suffer the little children and forbid them not, for such is the Kingdom of Heaven.'"

Eddie didn't need to look down at his worn Bible. He spoke from memory. "Forbid them not."

For just a moment, Charlie imagined Danny being with Jesus, but he quickly turned his thoughts to the kind of repairs he might be doing in the coming days.

Eddie went on to stress the need for special patience with the parents and the kids, and then, as he concluded, he invited the workers to rise and walk a few feet forward to kneel at the altar, where they would celebrate the Lord's Supper together.

The staff rose in unison, and Nora took Charlie's arm as they moved forward and knelt. Soft music played in the background--a children's choir singing "Amazing Grace." Charlie's knees were feeling the hardness of the concrete floor, and he hoped this wasn't going to take long.

Eddie stood on the inside of the altar, directly in front of the camp workers. Slowly, he read. "When the hour came, Jesus and his apostles reclined at the table. And he said to them, 'I have eagerly desired to eat this Passover with you before I suffer. For I tell you, I will not eat it again until it finds fulfillment in the kingdom of God.' After taking the cup, he gave thanks and said, 'Take this and divide it among you. For I tell you I will not drink again of the fruit of the vine until the kingdom of God comes.' And he took bread, gave thanks and broke it, and gave it to them, saying, 'This is my body given for you; do this in remembrance of me.' In the same way, after the supper he took the cup, saying, 'This cup is the new covenant of my blood, which is poured out for you.'"

As Charlie heard Eddie's footsteps approaching the Communion table to pick up the tray that held the bread and communion cup, his eyes fell upon the words carved in the front of the table. "In remembrance of me."

Eddie had just read those words, and now, here they were again. Charlie shifted his weight uncomfortably from one knee to the other, trying to think of something else. Even as he tried to forget the painful memories of his son, God seemed to be putting the memories of His son in their faces....never letting them forget it. Charlie thought, *I don't know how God does it. If I were God, I wouldn't allow this to happen. I wouldn't want people to keep on remembering the death of my son. Why is it so important to keep reviving the memory of the horrible death of Jesus?*

Eddie passed the bread and the cup so that each one could partake. As they were extended to Charlie, he could hear the children's voices, singing. "When we've been there ten thousand years, bright shining as the stars." Charlie received the bread and the cup.

The thought of the Son of God's broken body and shed blood brought to Charlie's mind Danny's broken body.

He was sweating and felt like he was drowning, and he nudged Nora and whispered breathlessly, "I've got to get out of here."

He pushed himself to his feet and started up the long aisle toward the door. The walls were closing in on him…fast. He fastened his eyes on the door, struggling to get to it. Then everything went dark.

CHAPTER THIRTY-FIVE

Everyone heard Charlie fall, unconscious, on the concrete floor. He had hit his head on the corner of a pew as he went down, and the nasty gash was bleeding heavily.

In a flash, Millie was beside him, grabbing tissues from her purse and pressing them on the cut to stop the flow of blood. Ralph called 911. Someone found paper towels in the bathroom and brought them to Millie. It was a bloody mess.

Charlie heard Nora's voice calling him from far away, "Charlie, Charlie, can you hear me?" He tried to sit up but several hands kept him down.

"What happened?"

"You fainted, Charlie, and you hit your head. There's an ambulance on the way."

"I think I'm okay," he said weakly. Nora helped him sit up, but she wouldn't let him stand. Looking down at his clothes and realizing someone was keeping pressure on his head, he asked, "What happened? I don't remember."

"Charlie, you passed out and hit your head."

His heart was racing, and he was breathing as if he had just run a footrace. He could hear a siren in the distance.

━┼╍ ╍┼━

By the time Charlie got to the hospital, the bleeding had subsided, but the doctors could tell from his clothes that he had lost a lot of blood.

Ralph had driven Millie and Nora to the hospital, and when they arrived at the Emergency Room the nurses had already removed Charlie's shirt and taken his vital signs.

The ER doctor looked over the EMT report and noted that Charlie's pulse rate was 160 and his blood pressure 175/95. Not good numbers.

The doctor ordered a suture kit, put on latex gloves as he focused on Charlie's wound. After using a local anesthetic, he prepared for the first stitch.

"Mr. Davis, I noticed they brought you here from Ridgeview Camp."

"Yes," Charlie answered as he winced a bit. "We just got here from Missouri Friday night. Our first time in North Carolina."

The doctor continued, his expert hands sewing the separated skin into place. "So, what were you doing when this happened--playing ball or something?"

"No, we were in the chapel. They told me I was at the altar when this happened."

"They told you? Don't you remember much of what you were doing before you fell?"

Charlie was a little embarrassed. "My wife told me that I got up from the altar and started down the aisle to leave the chapel. She said I fainted and hit my head on the corner of one of the benches."

The doctor was nearly finished with the sutures.

"Mr. Davis, I'm curious to know what made you pass out; you don't seem to be dehydrated. If you don't mind, I would like to take an EKG and see if there is anything going on with your heart."

Charlie raised his hand in protest, but Nora was nearby, listening.

"You should do it while he's here. I will never get him back here for it."

"Well, it won't take long. We'll do it before you leave."

The test was administered, and by the time the doctor returned with results, Charlie was sitting on the edge of the bed drinking orange juice from a paper cup and feeling better.

The doctor made no small talk. "Your EKG shows some irregular patterns, but I don't think it's anything serious."

Charlie and Nora relaxed.

"However, this report does indicate that we need to do a little more testing before we know for sure. I'm going to let you go today, but I want you to call this number tomorrow morning and schedule an echocardiogram." He took a business card from his clipboard and handed it to Nora.

"What's an echocardiogram?" Charlie asked.

"It's a test that will give us a more complete look at your heart and might help us figure out why you fainted. One thing for sure, we don't want you passing out and hitting your head like this again."

Charlie nodded as he slid off the side of the bed and took a couple steps. He was clear-headed and felt confident he could walk on his own, but Nora held his arm as they walked to the waiting room where Ralph and Millie were seated.

When they got back to the camp, most of the staff stood outside the chapel where Eddie had asked them to gather. They had been praying earnestly for Charlie. The whole group applauded as Charlie stepped out of the car. Nora reported the fifteen stitches, but neither she nor Charlie mentioned the irregular EKG.

After answering several questions and assuring everyone he was okay, Charlie realized he was hungry. Nora quickly led him to their cabin where he ate a light snack and took a couple of over-the-counter pain killers before laying down to rest. Nora spent the rest of the afternoon visiting with Ralph and Millie on the porch.

CHAPTER THIRTY-SIX

J D had just finished the morning message and Anna was waiting for him to finish up in his office when his phone rang. He immediately recognized Rudy Ferguson's voice. Rudy was an old buddy who once had been pastor in a neighboring town but was now an evangelist. JD hadn't heard from him in a while.

Rudy had been preaching in Charlotte when word reached the church that the staff at Ridgeview was requesting prayer for Charlie Davis, a volunteer at the camp. When Rudy heard the name, he knew it was JD's son, Charlie.

Rudy's voice bellowed into JD's ear. "Is this you, brother?"

"Yes, Rudy, my good brother. It's me. How are you?"

"Oh, JD, we are having a great time here in Charlotte. You should have seen what happened in church this morning. God was all over the place. I have never seen anything like it."

"Well, praise God," JD replied, wishing something like that had happened at his church.

"But that's not the reason for my call. I just heard they had an accident at the Ridgeview camp that involved your son, Charlie."

JD froze. "Oh, dear Lord. What happened, Rudy?"

"Charlie was rushed to the hospital. There was an accident in the chapel. It seems he fainted, hit his head on the edge of one of the benches, and gashed it open. I heard it took over fifty stitches to close it."

"My God, Rudy, it must have been horrible!"

"We heard here that he almost had to be given a blood transfusion because of the loss of blood. We're not sure, but we think he might be in the Intensive Care Unit. But rest assured, JD, we are going to keep praying for him here in the service tonight. I know he will be okay, praise God."

JD made his way out of his office to find Anna. She was still talking with some of her friends when JD told her what had happened. She quickly gathered up some of the women nearby and had an impromptu prayer meeting at the front of the church. It wasn't long until more than a dozen women were praying with her.

━◄⊹ ⊹►━

JD called the Asheville Medical Center and was told Charlie was not a patient. According to the receptionist, Charlie had been treated in the Emergency Room and sent home. JD wondered about the truth of what Rudy told him earlier. Rudy had a strong propensity to exaggerate, especially when it came to bad news. JD's next call was directly to Ridgeview.

The camp operator suggested JD try the phone in the shop. She explained that sometimes the phone could be heard from the cottage next door, and she encouraged JD to let it ring a while. JD was getting more impatient with each ring.

JD fidgeted and drummed his fingers across the yellow writing pad on his desk as the phone continued ringing. Inwardly, he was praying that somehow Charlie, Nora, or someone would hear the phone and pick up.

Finally an unfamiliar male voice answered. Ralph had gone to the shop to get a pair of pliers and heard the phone. He explained that Charlie was now home from the hospital and had never been in Intensive Care. JD, wanting more information, pressed Ralph, "Can I speak to Nora, my daughter-in-law?" Ralph asked JD to wait while he ran next door to get her.

Nora had just gotten Charlie settled in a recliner when she heard Ralph knock on the door, and she jogged next door to talk with JD.

"Nora, this is Dad. I just heard about Charlie. Tell me what happened and how he's doing." Nora told the whole story, telling about the special service in the chapel. She went on to say that Charlie tried to get away from the altar but had fallen in the aisle, hitting his head.

As JD listened, he began to think Charlie might be under conviction for not paying a tithe on the settlement.

"Nora, tell me honestly. Do you think he has been dealing with something spiritually? Do you think he is being disobedient and walking behind light?"

Nora hesitated, secretly praying that God would help her to not say anything she would later regret.

"No, Dad, I think it was just one of those things that happens. Maybe he was simply worn out from the long drive to get here."

Nora said nothing about the concerns she had about Charlie's heart. No need to upset anyone until they knew more. She didn't want to worry JD, and she certainly didn't want him showing up at Ridgeview.

━✦✦━

While Charlie was resting, twelve vans and four church buses, along with several cars, arrived sporadically at the campground. Nora could hear the sounds of excited children from her porch, where she sat reading her Bible. She looked up to see an eleven year old boy throwing a Frisbee with Roscoe, the camp dog, chasing after it. It reminded her of Danny and Spike. Just then, Charlie opened the screen door.

"I can't sleep," he announced as he stepped onto the porch. "I thought I might as well come out here and sit a while."

Nora pointed to the youngster and the dog playing with the Frisbee. Without a word, Charlie turned and walked back into the cottage. *Maybe Ridgeview isn't going to be such a big help after all,* he thought. *There are still reminders of Danny everywhere I look.*

CHAPTER THIRTY-SEVEN

The next morning, Charlie and Nora were walking up the asphalt path with Ralph and Millie just as the camp bell announced breakfast was being served. This morning, excited children and their mothers outnumbered the workers and volunteers.

Most of the boys had been too excited about a week of horseback riding, canoe races, fishing, and softball games to sleep. Even learning about the mandatory Bible classes didn't dampen their enthusiasm.

Many of the girls were looking forward to the same activities as the boys and wanted to form their own softball team and compete against them while many of the other girls were looking forward to making their own jewelry in art classes and painting each other's faces. All the kids were quickly learning how much fun camp would be.

The single moms smiled as their kids' excitement built. The week of fun they had promised had finally arrived, and they were anticipating the break from the heartbreak and grief. Nearly all of them were living in homes without dads.

Joe Wright gathered everyone together and waited patiently for the noisy buzz to die down before he spoke. Finally, he began his instructions.

"You received your camp program at registration yesterday. Please note that we have only thirty minutes until your first Bible class." Joe put his clipboard down on the table so he could use both hands for directions.

He pointed as he explained. "All boys, up to age eight, will be meeting outdoors near the flag pole. Girls to age eight will be under the trees down by the volleyball courts. Boys aged nine to twelve will meet down by the corral on the left side. The girls will meet on the other side of the corral. All boys ages thirteen to sixteen will be down by the camp swimming pool, and the girls will meet behind the dining hall. Your parents will be meeting off to the side here, where the camp workers are eating now."

The group dispersed, and Charlie and Ralph headed to the shop.

"Charlie, have you had much experience working on Chevy pickups with 4-wheel drive?"

"Yeah, I have worked on just about everything. Do you have one that needs attention?"

Ralph pointed around to the back side of the shop as he spoke, "I didn't say anything earlier, but come around behind the shop with me."

They walked around the building to the back. Almost hidden in the bushes was a blue 4X4 pick up that had been parked there for a long time from the looks of the foliage growth around it.

Charlie stopped in his tracks when he got a closer look. It looked almost identical to Danny's truck. It was blue, complete with mud flaps, just like Danny's. The color drained from Charlie's face.

Ralph kicked one of the front tires. "I've never worked on one of these engines before, but I'm hoping you can get it running."

Charlie put his hand to his head and stepped back. "I'm getting another headache--must be from that spill I took yesterday. If you don't mind, I'm going to go back to our place and get something for it." With that, Charlie turned and walked away.

***

"Charlie, you're white as a sheet," Nora said when Charlie walked through the door.

"I think I might need to take it easy a little while longer, Charlie told her as he walked toward the bedroom. "I'm just going to rest for a little while." She heard him sit on the bed and pull his boots off.

Without a word, she picked up her purse and went to the porch. Nora found the business card of the cardiology group that she had been given earlier at the hospital. She walked next door to the shop to make the call.

Nora didn't see Ralph, who was sitting on the floor in the back of the shop changing the tire on a golf cart. And Ralph didn't know Nora had come in until she started talking into the phone.

The receptionist who answered the phone was businesslike and asked about Charlie's symptoms. Nora explained what had happened the day before when Charlie had been rushed to the medical center. She explained how he had fainted and hit his head. She went into detail, telling how the doctor had some concerns with Charlie's heart and asked them to call for an appointment with the cardiology group.

Nora made the appointment for Charlie and was cautioned by the receptionist to call 911 if she felt Charlie was in an emergency situation. She left without realizing Ralph was within earshot and had heard her end of the conversation and the mention of concerns about Charlie's heart.

Nora didn't want to disturb Charlie's rest, so she went directly from the shop to the chapel for the daily morning worship service. As the campers entered the tabernacle, most of the younger children sat with their mothers while the teens sat with others near their own age.

After a few choruses were sung, Joe introduced Eddie as their camp speaker for the coming week.

Eddie opened his Bible, leaned forward, and spoke into the microphone, "And a little child will lead them."

That opening scripture from Isaiah 11 got the attention of the parents, and the small children smiled and looked up to see what he meant. Eddie announced that this phrase from the Bible would be the theme for the coming week. His remarks were directed to everyone, but especially to the parents. He asked them to tune in to what God might say to them--even through their children.

Charlie lay with his eyes closed, still unsettled from seeing the pickup behind the shop. He wanted to sleep and forget it all. He was starting to drift off, but he heard the campers and staff singing choruses through his open window, and he heard Eddie's opening words, "A child shall lead them."

My child is gone, he thought. *Does God mean for me to die and follow Danny? What does it mean for a child to lead an adult?* Finally, he drifted off to sleep.

The clang of the big bell roused Charlie from his nap. As he awoke, his first conscious thought was *and a child shall lead them.*

"Hi, sleepy head," Nora teased as she came into the room. "Did you have a good nap?"

Charlie nodded, "I don't know what happened. Guess I'm still tired from the long drive out here."

Nora walked over to the dresser, picked up her brush, and ran it through her hair. "While you were sleeping, I went ahead and made an appointment for your heart test. I think it's called an echocardiogram."

"Yeah, and I don't see the reason for doing that. They only want to get more money from our insurance."

"No, Charlie. You are not going to ignore this! The doctor said there was a reason you passed out, and we are going to follow through and get to the bottom of it."

Charlie tuned her out, put on his boots, and the two of them started up the asphalt trail to the dining hall.

From where they sat in the section of the dining hall set aside for staff, Charlie could easily see the activity going on in the kids' eating area.

He noticed one boy who seemed to be around eight years old. Unlike the other children, he wasn't laughing and having fun. He sat alone, picking at his food. He was a cute kid, but something was clearly wrong. Charlie wondered about the child and hoped he would be able to loosen up and enjoy being at camp.

Charlie was feeling better by the time lunch was over, so over Nora's objections, he headed to the shop with Ralph.

One of the things that needed immediate attention was a golf cart that sometimes worked just fine and then would suddenly die without warning. Since it was battery powered, Ralph felt certain it was an electrical problem, and Ralph had brought with him a tool to check the connectivity of auto electrical circuits. Although Charlie had never tinkered with golf carts, he was able to diagnose the problem and tape the two loose wires together in short order.

The afternoon heat was stifling, so Charlie and Ralph were grateful when Nora appeared with a pitcher of ice cold lemonade. After finishing his drink and setting the glass down on the work bench, Charlie wiped his mouth and announced, "I think I have the problem fixed on this cart. But I want to give it a spin to make sure."

Ralph nodded toward the asphalt path that led down the hill and away from the dining room. "If you take that path and follow it on down the hill, you'll come to the recreation area. It's about a quarter mile."

Ralph picked up a wrench, walked over to another golf cart he was repairing as he spoke over his shoulder to Charlie, "Why don't you take it on down there, make a circle and then come on back. There are some holes in the trail and if there is a problem, it will show up when you drive across those rough places. Be careful."

Charlie slid behind the wheel, turned the key, pressed the accelerator pedal and took off down the hill. Looking off in the west, he noticed the sky was darkening a bit. He didn't know a lot about the weather in North Carolina, but he suspected a thunderstorm was about to roll in.

Ralph was right, Charlie decided. There were rough places in the trail with lots of ruts, but the golf cart worked perfectly in spite of the bumps and jostling. Charlie was pleased.

When he got to the bottom of the winding path, Charlie saw three ball fields, all with games in progress. The younger boys played on one of the diamonds, the older boys played on another, and the girls had a game going on the third.

The cart trail circled all three ball fields, and Charlie stopped to watch the younger boys for a while. It brought back memories of Danny's games when he was a child. Charlie decided he needed to get his mind off Danny, and was about to drive away when he noticed the lonely boy from the dining room was next in line to bat. He decided to wait and watch him take his turn.

The boy at the plate took a walk, and the boy from the dining room moved to the batter's box. Charlie could hear the other boys yelling for the kid. "Let's go, Clay. Get a hit! You can do it, Clay."

The bases were loaded, and Clay stood in the batter's box with the bat held just above his shoulder.

Come on, Clay, Charlie cheered silently. *Be the hero!*

The pitcher delivered the first pitch. Ball one. The second pitch was inside. Ball two. The next pitch was right down the middle, but Clay swung too early, and the ball sailed wide of third base. Foul ball. The pitcher threw another ball. The count stood at 3 and 1. If the pitcher threw another ball, Clay would walk and the winning run would cross the plate. Clay decided to hope for another ball rather than risk swinging the bat. The next pitch came in just off the plate, but the umpire called a strike.

The intensity of the game was higher than ever as Clay prepared for the pitch that would probably end the game. As his new teammates yelled encouragement to him, the nervous pitcher took a moment to talk to the first baseman, who had walked over to the pitcher's mound to strategize.

Charlie was the first to hear the barely audible clap of thunder in the distance. The second clap was louder, and Clay stiffened, dropped his bat, and tore off his helmet as he ran toward the opening in the fence by the backstop.

Clay was clearly terrified. He didn't say anything or even look at anyone. He ran from the ball diamond as fast as he could up the steep hill and back toward the camp.

Charlie jammed the accelerator on the golf cart to catch up with the child. Charlie hollered, "Hey buddy, let me give you a lift!"

At first, Clay didn't say anything, he was running as fast as he could. When he saw Charlie rumbling along beside him in the golf cart, he slowed for a moment, and then, much to Charlie's surprise, wanted to get in.

He was nearly out of breath. "I have to find my mom!" Charlie sensed the panic in his voice, and he was on the verge of tears. The boy slid onto the vinyl seat beside Charlie.

Just ahead of them lightning flashed, followed by another loud clap of thunder. When the little boy saw the lightning and heard the thunder, he screamed and threw his arms around Charlie's waist, hiding his face in Charlie's shoulder. Realizing the child was panicked, Charlie held him close as the first rain drops spattered against the plastic windshield of the cart.

Charlie drove with one hand on the wheel and the other arm around the terrified child. There was a shed just off the trail up ahead where the riding mowers were kept. When Charlie saw the door was open and that the shed was empty, he quickly wheeled in. The front of the storm was kicking up dust, leaves, and small limbs. Charlie decided they could ride out the storm in the old shed.

Clay's eyes were closed, his face buried in Charlie's blue shop shirt. The force of the storm was coming in the opposite direction, so Charlie reached down and set the brake. Wrapping both arms around the frightened child, Charlie could feel him shaking.

Charlie tried to console the child. "Hey, pal, we're safe here. My name is Charlie." Another lightning strike and a clap of thunder and more shuddering and tightening of his hands onto Charlie.

After a few moments, the little boy said, between sobs, "My name is Clay, and I need to find my mom. Do you know where she is?"

"No, I don't know where she is, but I'm sure we can find her when the storm lets up a little. When we can, we'll drive on up the hill. Don't worry, we'll find her. Are you worried about her?"

Clay didn't respond right away as the intensity of the rain picked up. Charlie thought he heard hail hitting the old wood-shingled roof.

"No, I just want her!" Charlie kept his arms around the little boy.

"That's okay. We'll find her soon." Then, trying to calm Clay, he asked, "Where are you from? Do you live in Charlotte?"

Clay responded with a quick nod.

"Have you ever been in a storm like this?"

The boy sat in terrified silence for a few moments, then spoke in a sobbing voice. "Yes--yes, it killed my Dad!"

Charlie tightened his arms around Clay. "Can you tell me what happened?"

The only sound was the beating rain on roof. "When did it happen?"

Clay wiped away a tear. "Last summer at my birthday party. It was just like this!"

"We're safe here."

Clay was beginning to relax. But each time he heard a clap of thunder, he flinched. Charlie wondered if he should press for more information on what had happened to Clay's dad.

"Clay, can you tell me what happened at your birthday party?"

The boy was thinking hard, forming his response. Turning his head to look out at the rain, he said, "It was last summer at my birthday party. Mom said I could have seven of my best friends for my party, because that was the number of my age--seven. Dad said he would hit some flies and grounders to us. All my best friends at school are good ball players. I told them to bring their ball gloves with them to the party."

Charlie nodded. He could feel Clay relaxing as he talked.

"My dad made hamburgers on the patio. After we ate, I wanted to go outside so Dad could hit some flies and grounders to us, but Dad said it looked like it was about to storm. But I just kept begging Dad until he said okay, we could do it, but we would have to come back inside if it started raining."

Charlie listening closely as Clay continued.

"So, I got the bat and ball for Dad to use, and we all went outside. My dad can hit them higher than anyone else!"

Charlie nodded and noticed that Clay spoke of his dad in the present tense.

"It got really dark, but it hadn't started raining yet. Dad hit one almost over our heads. I ran back, keeping my eyes on the ball, and I caught it! I think I heard my dad yell, 'Great catch, Clay!' Then a big lightning came down right where my dad was."

Charlie tried to imagine what it might have been like for the little boy who was clinging to him. When it felt safe to ask, Charlie spoke softly, "Can you tell me what happened next?

"When the lightning came all the way to the ground, all of my buddies and I got knocked to the ground too. It was really strong. When we got up, my dad was still on the ground. My mom came out of the house and we all ran over to him, and there was smoke coming out of his clothes. I tried to wake him up 'cause I thought he was knocked out. I thought the lightning had knocked him out!"

Clay went on, determined to tell the whole story. "My mom tried to get my dad to talk to her. She was crying and even screaming at him, but he didn't move! She yelled for me to go call 911, and I ran as fast as I could and called them. The lady asked what happened and I told her and said my dad couldn't wake up. She asked for my address, and I told her. She told me help would be there soon, so I went back outside to help my mom wake him up."

Clay was lost in his story and rushed on. "My mom kept pressing on his chest, and she was crying and screaming. Then we heard the sirens, and an ambulance, a fire truck, and a police car all came to our house. These policemen came running into our backyard. They pulled my mom back from my dad, and then they started yelling at him to wake up! They opened up his shirt and started to do something, but then some other policeman told me and my friends to go in the house. We went inside but we looked out the window, and they put Dad on a stretcher, and—and—he was dead, and I won't ever see him again."

Charlie could feel tears on his own face as he heard the tragic story told by the eight-year-old in his arms. The rain was letting up, and Clay had stopped shaking. He looked up into Charlie's face and saw his tears.

"I'm sorry I made you cry, mister."

Charlie was embarrassed, "It's okay, I'm not crying. I think maybe some rain blew in my face."

Clay, satisfied Charlie was okay, had more to tell. "Since that happened, everything has gone wrong. I know it's my fault, because if we hadn't gone outside, it wouldn't have happened. I made my dad do it. Every time I hear a storm, it's like it happens to me again."

"Have you told your mom how scared you are of storms?"

"Oh, she knows all right. She took me to a counselor a bunch of times."

"And what did the counselor say to you?"

"She said that it was okay for me to feel this way. She said I should ask someone to stay with me when it storms and its okay to tell them what happened to my dad. She said it would help if I did that."

Charlie reached out and put his hand on Clay's shoulder. "Well, I'm glad I could be here for you today. I hope it helped that we could talk."

Clay smiled as he looked up at Charlie, "I think I feel better now."

The two continued to talk for another thirty minutes, and they both became increasingly comfortable, as though they had known each other for a long time. Soon, the rain stopped, and they were back on the trail, driving up the hill to the dining hall.

When Clay's mother saw him in the cart, she ran toward them. After hugging her son, Clay told how Charlie had protected him from the storm.

She turned and spoke to Charlie, "You will never know how much I appreciate you watching over him. He doesn't handle storms very well."

Smiling, Charlie nodded his head toward Clay, "I was glad to do it. I think I've made a new friend."

After dinner and the evening chapel service, Charlie, Nora, Ralph and Millie were sitting on the porch of the Davis cottage.

"Man, that was quite a storm today. I heard it knocked out the power down in Asheville, and they are still trying to replace the transformers that were hit."

When Ralph mentioned the storm, Charlie was prompted to tell them about his encounter with Clay down by the ball diamonds. He told them about the long conversation they had while they waited out the storm in the shed.

"I imagine he'll be a little spooked by thunder and lightning until he goes through a few more storms like we had today," Ralph said.

"Yes," Charlie agreed, "His counselor told him it was best not to run away, and that he should find someone to be with and not be afraid to tell about his dad being struck by lightning."

Nora had listened to Charlie's experience and added thoughtfully, "That counselor gave good advice, I think. We all have storms in our lives, and it's good to have someone we can talk to about it. "

CHAPTER THIRTY-EIGHT

N ora thumbed through a magazine after Charlie was led back to the examination room.

Charlie answered health questions and had a blood pressure check before he was instructed to remove his shirt for the exam. A technician came in and taped several electrodes on his chest, and a clip was placed on his right index finger to measure his oxygen level.

Next, he was asked to step up on the treadmill in the room, and a blood pressure cuff was wrapped around his arm. It was explained that his blood pressure would be monitored while the test was conducted.

When everything was set, a different doctor came in and the test began. The treadmill started slowly, and after a few minutes of warm-up, the technicians began to speed up the pace. A large X-ray arm was in front of Charlie's chest, and Charlie realized the angle of the treadmill was changing so that it felt as if he was walking uphill at a fast clip. He gripped the sides of the treadmill tightly as he walked faster. It wasn't long until he began to feel lightheaded and his legs began to feel like Jell-O.

One of the technicians noticed the change in his condition.

"Mr. Davis, are you okay?"

"I feel a little weak," Charlie answered. "Maybe we'd better stop."

Immediately, the treadmill was shut down. The technicians took him, one on each arm, and sat him in a nearby chair. Trickles of sweat ran down both sides of his face.

One of the techs nodded to the other, and she left the room. Soon, there were two doctors attending to Charlie, one listening to Charlie's heart with a stethoscope while the other examined the just-completed test results.

Both doctors had questions for Charlie. There were questions about his symptoms and more questions about his parents. Both doctors wanted to know the detailed history of heart issues in the Davis family.

Even though Charlie felt woozy, he recognized the concern on the physicians' faces. Soon, he was given a drink of water and told to get dressed and join Nora in the doctor's office where a nurse had taken her.

"Mr. Davis, according to the findings of the echocardiogram, you have an abnormal and irregular heart pattern that will need to be treated."

"What does that mean? I have never had problems with my heart."

Doctor Strickler removed his glasses and explained. "You have an abnormality in the electrical impulse that affects your heart-beat." The doctor leaned back and pointed to a colorful picture of a heart on the wall. "This condition can be undetected until it takes you quite suddenly." The doctor leaned forward in his seat. "Mr. Davis, some people call this condition the Widow maker."

Feeling vulnerable, Charlie asked, "What causes this to happen?"

"We aren't quite sure why this happens; there could be any number of reasons. Sometimes it occurs because of head trauma. There are also other scientific reports that show it can be brought on by extreme stress. One thing we do know for sure is that it seems to be run in families. Is your father living?"

Charlie nodded.

"Does he have a pacemaker?"

"No, I know for sure that he doesn't."

The doctor held up Charlie's file. "Based on this, I advise you to tell him about our findings. Ask him to get checked for this problem, and soon."

He tossed the file onto his desk. "In addition, just to be safe, I suggest you have *your* children checked. Regardless of age, this condition can be exacerbated by stress. Have you had any unusual or extreme stress in your life lately?"

Charlie leaned back in his chair. "Heck no, Doctor. I'm retired and it's like I'm on vacation every day." Both Charlie and the doctor laughed.

Nora had sat quietly, listening to the conversation.

"Doctor," she asked, "could the death of our son have anything to do with Charlie's symptoms?"

Dr. Strickler looked at Charlie. "When did this happen?"

Charlie waved his hand dismissively, "Oh, that happened months ago."

"Well, let me tell you that the death of a child ranks as one of the absolute worst stressors any parent can experience. And, yes, it could definitely be a contributing factor to your heart problems. Can you tell me how your son died?"

Charlie was looking at the floor. "It was an accident. His truck went off the road, down a steep ravine, and crashed."

"I'm so sorry. Did he fall asleep?"

Nora, reached for a tissue before she answered. "We don't know."

The doctor looked at Charlie's chart a few seconds and then broke the silence. "Had a doctor ever said your son had an irregular heart beat or heart abnormalities of any kind?"

"You think our son might have had heart problems?"

"Yes, it's very possible." He paused and looked at the top page of data on Charlie's file. "Even probable, given the fact that the cause of his accident cannot be determined. Do you know if your son was under any stress or had received bad news just before his accident?"

Charlie and Nora shook their heads, and Nora spoke. "He was a good kid, a straight A student. He was popular, captain of the football team, and he had a steady girlfriend that we loved. He never gave us a moment's trouble. He was a happy kid in a happy home. I can't think of anything in his life that would cause him stress."

"I would like very much to know all that happened to him in the twenty four hours prior to his accident." The doctor looked first at Nora, then at Charlie.

"For now, Charlie, you need to have a pacemaker put in as soon as possible. It's a rather benign procedure."

He used the model heart on his desk to demonstrate how wires would be implanted in two of his arteries that would go to the inner chambers of his heart. The wires would emit an electrical impulse that would be powered from a special battery pack that would be implanted just under his collar bone on his left side.

"You will be sedated but semi-awake during the procedure. You won't have much pain, but you'll stay in the hospital at least twenty-four hours so we can monitor how your heart is responding to the pacemaker."

Charlie and Nora were in a daze as the arrangements were made for surgery the following day. The doctor's assistant gave a few further instructions before they left.

"You won't be able to use your left arm for a few days, Mr. Davis, while the incision heals. Mrs. Davis, you'll need to do the driving until he's back to regular activity."

Nora nodded numbly. "I can do that."

⟞⟝⟞

That night, Nora and Charlie found it nearly impossible to fall asleep. Side by side, they stared at the shadows on the ceiling. Finally, Nora broke the silence.

"You awake?"

"Yeah."

"I've been thinking about what the doctor said to us today."

"Me too."

"Do you think there could have been something we didn't know about? Something that upset Danny and maybe that's why he missed the turn?"

"I wish I knew."

As Charlie turned on his side, he thought he felt his heart skip a beat or two. He waited a few seconds, holding his breath, as it fluttered and started beating normally again.

I'm not sure I would care if it stopping beating completely, Charlie thought. *I could be with Danny instead of missing him every minute.*

Ralph insisted on driving the Davises to the hospital the next morning and Millie was coming along to support Nora, so the four of them left early before breakfast.

After Charlie had been taken back for the procedure, Nora realized his parents hadn't been informed about the pacemaker. She needed to make the call.

"Dad, it's me."

"Is everything okay, Nora?"

"Yes, everything's fine, but I wanted to let you know the latest. When Charlie fell and hit his head the other day, and he went to the Emergency Room, they thought they detected some irregularities with his heart, so they did some further testing yesterday. To make a long story short, we are at the hospital this morning, and Charlie is having a pacemaker implanted in his chest.

"Nora, are you sure those doctors there know what they're doing?" JD's voice was loud and demanding.

"Yes, Dad, they are very good doctors; most of them trained at Duke." She paused, bracing for pushback from JD. "Anyway, Charlie just went to surgery about ten minutes ago. He will be in there for about an hour. I thought you and Mom would want to know so you can pray for him."

Nora couldn't think of a tactful way to bring up JD's health, so she just asked him quick and to the point.

"Dad, have you ever had any troubling symptoms with your own heart?"

"Of course not. I've never had a minute's problem with my heart. Praise God."

"Well, I think you should know that the doctors told us Charlie's condition is one that often runs in families." She paused a moment, letting her words sink in.

"They told us to mention it to you so that you could have your doctor examine you for this."

JD swallowed hard. He could hardly believe what she was telling him.

"Dad, they think this heart condition is especially susceptible to stress. When sudden stress comes on a person who has this condition, it can cause the heart to stop beating--without any warning. I know this is hard for you to hear, Dad, but the doctor insisted that you know about the importance of getting checked."

JD got off the phone thinking about the fluttering feeling he had experienced in his chest recently. As he thought back, he realized it had, indeed, come during times of intense stress, especially during Danny's funeral when the dog fight caused a scene. He had never told anyone, not even Anna.

He leaned back in the leather chair and wondered if it could be true. *If this heart problem is for real, and if it really does run in families, could it be that Danny had it?* He closed his eyes and prayed silently, hoping that he was not responsible for passing this down his family tree.

CHAPTER THIRTY-NINE

When Charlie came to after surgery, his left arm was in a sling and was tightly secured to his chest. He was wheeled to the cardiac wing where his heart would be monitored for at least twenty-four hours.

Soon after he was settled into his room, Nora, Millie, and Ralph were allowed to see him for a few minutes. Charlie had a light meal, and after a short visit, he was ready for a nap, so his visitors headed back to the camp, assured that Charlie would be fine.

Two hours later, when Charlie awakened from his nap, his head was completely clear. He could hear a male voice nearby, and realized he was in a double room divided by a cloth partition. The voice he heard was his roommate talking on the phone.

Charlie could hear only one side of the conversation, but it was obvious that something bad had happened. It seemed the other patient was talking about the death of his son, Randy, who had been killed in a bloody battle. The boy was a soldier and his body was being returned to Dover Airbase.

When Charlie fully understood that the death of the man's son was very recent, he broke out in a cold sweat. He knew exactly what this stranger, only a few feet from him, was going through.

Charlie remained completely still. He thought he heard the man crying, but wasn't sure. He started to speak, then decided to remain quiet a while longer.

A few minutes later, he heard a female voice--maybe a nurse--speaking to the other patient.

"I've called for the chaplain to come and talk with you for a while," she offered. "Your heart monitor indicates you are under extreme stress right now."

Before long, Charlie heard the chaplain come into the room and what sounded like a chair being scooted across the floor. Charlie felt like he was an accidental eavesdropper on a private conversation, but he remained silent while the chaplain and the patient in the other bed talked.

The young soldier was only 19 years old and had been killed in action. The news of the boy's death had hit the dad hard; so hard that it resulted in a heart attack.

As Charlie listened, he thought, *What are the odds I would end up in a room with another guy whose son had been killed?*

It was a surreal experience to be witnessing another father's raw pain, and Charlie completely identified with the man's emotion.

There was no conversation between the chaplain and the patient for a full minute, but then the chaplain spoke.

"I know just how you feel, because I lost my own dad two years ago."

Charlie felt himself growing tense. *The situations are nothing alike. He doesn't know how it feels.* Charlie's hands were clinched into fists as he heard the chaplain going on and on about his father.

Immediately, a nurse appeared at Charlie's bedside. "Mr. Davis, are you okay?"

Charlie's face was flushed. "Yeah, sure, I think I'm okay."

The nurse straightened his bed sheets, "Well, we have been watching you on the monitor at the nurse's station. You're heart rate is of concern to us right now."

Charlie shook off her concern, but the nurse wasn't convinced.

"We'll watch it for a little while longer, but we may need to call the doctor to prescribe something to help you relax."

She left the room just as the chaplain said goodbye to the other patient and left.

"Hey, do you mind if I pull back this bed sheet between us?" Charlie asked his roommate.

"No, go ahead. Name here is Ben Smith."

"I'm Charlie Davis." Charlie reached over with his right hand to pull back the cloth partition. Unfamiliar with the bed controls, he pushed several buttons until he found the one to raise his head to a more comfortable position.

When Charlie rose up to where he could see Ben, he swung his legs around so that he faced Ben's bed.

"I heard what you said to the chaplain." He paused a moment. "I'm very sorry to hear about your son."

"I just found out yesterday. It feels like a nightmare I can't wake up from. Like maybe those uniformed officers didn't really appear at my door, or maybe they made a mistake and it was some other boy."

At the nurse's station, Lou, the nurse who was caring for both men, had just returned to her desk. She could easily hear them talking through the intercom system that connected the patient rooms with the nurses' station. Charlie was unaware that he had accidentally pushed the call button when he was trying to raise the head of his bed.

Lou started to press the response button to ask Charlie what he needed, but Dr. Strickler was nearby and he raised his hand and motioned for her to wait.

Both men were his patients, and he knew their stories. He placed his hand over Lou's and whispered, "Not yet."

Charlie and Ben made small talk at first, exchanging information about where they were from, how long they had been married, what they did for a living.

Then Ben started talking about his son. His face grew red, and tears spilled down his cheeks. His shoulders began to heave up and down as he sobbed.

Charlie turned his face away, trying to think of something else. He briefly thought about getting up and leaving the room, or at least requesting to be moved, but then it came to him that he might have been put in this time and this place to identify with this man who had also lost his son. Maybe it was what JD always called "a God thing."

As Ben continued to talk about his son, Dr. Strickler and Lou listened. The doctor also kept a close eye on the heart monitors of both patients. Their heart rates had spiked when they started talking, but as the conversation progressed, their rates slowly returned to within normal ranges.

As Charlie shared about Danny, he was on the verge of tears several times, but he managed to hold them in check. But when he looked into the eyes of the other grief-stricken dad, he could see Ben's tears as he openly grieved for Charlie's loss. All at once, Charlie felt permission to allow his tears to be seen too and to let Ben share in his pain. Charlie surprised himself as he freely let his tears drip from his chin onto the white hospital sheets.

Dr. Strickler smiled as he watched the monitors track Ben's and Charlie's heart patterns. It seemed miraculous that both of their patterns returned to normal after they discovered and shared their mutual nightmares.

Strickler said, mostly to himself, but Lou heard it too, "Sorrow shared is sorrow halved."

He looked at Lou and said, "You ladies already know how to do this, but most guys have a hard time allowing themselves to go there."

Lou smiled and nodded. "You know, Doctor, I think these two have just now discovered what you just said. They are sharing their sorrow."

CHAPTER FORTY

Charlie awakened the next morning from the best sleep he'd had in months. Dr. Strickler came by and gave his final instructions: "Keep the sling on for forty-eight hours; do not get the incision wet for at least three days; no driving for seven days."

He handed Charlie a copy of the instructions in printed form, and said, "There's one more thing I want you to consider."

"What's that?"

"I think you will help yourself and enjoy better heart health if you could find a way to share your feelings with others. You are the kind of man who will benefit from a support group. I think you and your wife would do well in a group with other parents who have lost a child."

"I'll think about it, Doctor.

Ben was awake in the bed next to Charlie's when Nora, Millie, and Ralph arrived to take Charlie home, and Charlie was worried that his roommate might say something about Danny's death. He wasn't ready for Ralph and Millie to hear about Danny quite yet.

Charlie barely said goodbye to Ben as the nurse wheeled him out of the room and to the car, but his secret remained intact. Charlie also felt some guilt, because it seemed he was leaving behind a man who was drowning in a sea of grief.

When Charlie got back to the camp cottage, he was ready for a nap. He took it easy for the rest of the day. In fact, he planned to take it easy for the next several days, since he couldn't go back to work. He half-enjoyed simply sitting on the porch, listening to the sounds of the frogs and crickets. He could also hear the music and everything being said in the nearby chapel services.

After a couple of days, though, he began to grow a little restless, so he ventured over to the shop next door to see what Ralph was up to. Ralph was doing fine, but said he would be glad to see Charlie back whenever he was ready.

Charlie, feeling a bit more adventurous, noticed the golf cart nearby. He picked up the key as he spoke.

"The doctor said I couldn't drive a car, but he didn't say anything about a golf cart. I think I'll go for a little ride and get some air."

Charlie knew Nora would not approve, but he settled himself into the cart and headed down the path that led to the ball fields. He loved a good game, and thought he could pass the time as a spectator.

Hardly anyone noticed when Charlie stopped the cart under the shade of a tree about thirty yards behind the screened backstop. He was sitting on the cart, watching the game, when Clay walked up.

"Hi, Mr. Charlie, remember me?

"Sure, I remember you, Clay. How's the game going?"

"We're ahead by five runs, and I hit a double that knocked in two of them."

"Way to go, Clay! I wish I had been here to see it!"

"It's okay. I'll be up again in a little while."

Clay walked around to the other side of the cart, "Is it okay if I sit here until I'm up to bat?"

Charlie patted the black vinyl as an invitation. "Yeah, sit right down. Looks like it's going to be a real nice day today."

Clay settled on the seat, "Yeah. My mom said I should apologize to you because of what happened the other day and to thank you for taking care of me in that bad storm."

Charlie reached over with his good arm and made a playful brush across the top of Clay's ball cap. "Not a problem, buddy. I was glad I could be there for you. I'm glad we didn't get soaking wet."

Clay started to grin, but then a serious expression covered his face.

"I think I am getting a little bit better. Mom said that I just needed to try and face the storms, not run away from them. So, I decided the next time I hear thunder, I'll try to find someone to be with--someone like you!"

Clay smiled as he said, "When I was with you, it didn't seem as bad as the other times I heard thunder. I told my mom that I was going to try to find a friend to be with me whenever the storms come next time."

"Clay, you're up next," someone called from the ball field.

Clay slid off the seat and headed to the diamond. He yelled over his shoulder as he ran away, "Thanks again, Mr. Charlie."

Charlie watched as Clay ran back to his teammates. He played Clay's words over in his mind. *The next time I hear thunder, I'll try to find someone to be with—someone like you!*

Clay's words, coupled with his conversation with Ben, were percolating in Charlie's mind as he drove the cart back. He couldn't escape the similarities, even though one was mature and the other was young. Both were trying to overcome their worst nightmares.

When Charlie got back to the shop, Ralph had already gone to the dining hall for the supper. Charlie parked the cart and went to find Nora. He was ready to eat.

CHAPTER FORTY-ONE

After dinner, Nora asked Charlie to join her for the final chapel service of the week. He declined, saying he could hear just as well from the rocker on the front porch. The heat was stifling, and all the windows in the chapel were open.

Nora went on with the others, and Charlie settled into the rocking chair. In his short time here, he had come to love the Carolinas. He loved this camp, and the way the sun descended slowly behind the trees each evening. He loved the sounds of the woods nearby as he lingered on the porch watching the sun disappear.

Charlie heard Joe giving out the final awards to the campers, and was confident that Joe would make sure every kid received some kind of award or recognition. Charlie smiled when he heard Clay's name announced along with the names of his teammates. Their team had won first place.

After fifteen minutes of music--most of it camp choruses— Eddie began his message, the theme of which was "How to Overcome Your Worst Nightmare."

Eddie told the story of St. Peter, the disciple who denied Jesus, and explained how he had betrayed Jesus not just once but three times. He acted out the scene of the betrayal as though he were on stage. He gathered up six hymnals and chorus sheets, quickly stacking them on the platform as though they were coals that comprised a fire. The children paid rapt attention as their imaginations created a fire.

He again dramatized the situation where Jesus was being falsely accused. Then, he told how the friends of Jesus were threatened too. He played it up when he saw the children identifying with St. Peter. These children had also experienced moments when they felt threatened and had done or said whatever was necessary to survive.

Eddie's voice rose as he acted out the part of the maid who accused Peter of being a friend of Jesus. Then he told about the three denials, the betrayals and lies.

When Eddie came to the third denial of Peter, he mimicked the sound of a rooster crowing and emphasized the pain and disappointment Peter felt when he violated his own conscience by swearing he didn't even know Jesus.

He told of Jesus being falsely accused while Peter stayed away and watched it happen. Then he quickly described the crucifixion of Jesus.

As Charlie listened from his porch, Eddie told of the resurrection of Jesus and finally how the disciples had returned to their work as fishermen. He dramatized how they fished all night but caught nothing. Then, he told how Jesus was on the lake shore preparing a fire and cooking breakfast. Eddie told how Peter felt when he knew it was Jesus who was calling him from the shore.

Eddie reminded everyone that Peter had lied about knowing Jesus three times, and as Peter sat across from Jesus at the fire, Jesus asked Peter if he loved him. He asked three times.

"Why do you suppose Jesus asked Peter this question three times?"

One of the children in the crowd spoke out, "Because he lied three times."

Eddie explained that the fire on which Jesus was cooking the fish was exactly the kind of fire that Peter was warming himself by when he lied--a fire made up of coals, of charcoal.

Eddie told of Jesus forgiving Peter for lying, and Charlie, still listening from his porch, thought how different this message was from the messages his dad, JD, liked to emphasize in his sermons. JD talked more about God's punishment of burning in hell for lying or committing other sins rather than God's forgiveness.

"If Jesus hadn't talked to Peter about the lie he told three times, what do you think would have gone through Peter's mind every time he heard the number three or smelled the smoke of a charcoal fire?" Eddie's question hung in the air for a few seconds, then he continued.

"What are you trying to run from?" Eddie asked. "You can face your greatest pain and be free from memories that you're trying to run from. It always helps to tell God about these things. I invite you, both mothers and children, to come to the altar to kneel and pray to God. You can have a conversation with Jesus much like the conversation St. Peter had with him."

The piano played softly, and Charlie thought he heard the scuffle of footsteps, probably those coming forward to pray.

"Just come here to Jesus and tell him the things you are afraid of, the things you think about late at night, the things that keep you awake. Tell him even your worst thoughts," Eddie encouraged. "A counselor or pastor will pray with you if you like. Whether alone or with someone, talk about your worst and most painful thoughts. Don't be afraid to lean into your pain; Jesus will be here to help you."

Charlie considered Eddie's words. His own worst nightmare was losing Danny. Allowing himself to think about the trip to Devil's Elbow that foggy morning was just too much to face. Would it be too much to bear if he revisited that nightmare? He had tried so hard to forget that awful scene. He had tried so hard to forget what had happened on that awful night. *What if I was wrong to move away from Ladner? What if I was wrong to make Nora deny we ever had a son?* Charlie was beginning to doubt the choices he had made.

After leaving the chapel, Nora walked back to their cottage, thinking about facing her pain. She felt it was time to talk about Danny with Charlie.

Charlie was still on the porch, and was the first to speak. "How did it go?"

"Eddie spoke about the importance of facing our pain, facing our worst nightmares." She sat in the rocker next to Charlie.

"Eddie invited people to come forward who wanted to pray about the things that were haunting them, the things that had caused them their worst pain. Quite a few went forward, but I wasn't sure what to do. I finally decided to go forward and pray too."

Charlie quit rocking and sat staring straight ahead.

"Charlie, I know I promised I wouldn't say anything about Danny's death, but..." She stopped to measure each word carefully, "I am dying inside from carrying Danny's death around without anyone to talk to."

Charlie made no response.

"I wish we could tell someone what happened to us."

Charlie thought she was going to say more, but they heard footsteps, and through the darkness, they saw a man walking toward their porch. It was Eddie.

CHAPTER FORTY-TWO

"Eddie, is that you?" Nora called out as cheerfully as she could manage.

"Yeah, it's me. I wanted to see how Charlie is doing and say goodbye. I'll be leaving in the morning."

"Sorry I missed your last service, Eddie. I just thought I would stay here tonight and follow doctor's orders and take it easy for a while." Gesturing toward the chapel, he said, "Besides, I can hear the music and sermons from right here in my chair."

"Eddie, I thought you had an excellent message tonight. I'm sure it helped a lot of moms and kids." Nora glanced at Charlie. "It was a message both children and adults can benefit from. Even some of the volunteers who serve here."

Eddie nodded. "Yes, everyone has pain to deal with at some point in life."

Eddie seemed relaxed and reflective as he leaned against the post. "I've noticed that a lot of folks have pain and regrets they want to bury, hoping they will just go away." He paused, comfortable with the silence.

"The thing is, though, pain and regret have a 100 percent resurrection rate. We can't change or heal what we don't acknowledge."

The words hung there, between Charlie and Nora, as they thought about their son's death and how they had tried to run from it.

"Eddie, when you say these things have a 100 percent resurrection rate, what do you mean by that?" Charlie asked.

"Well, those painful things take up a lot of room inside a person's head. They need to be dealt with, and suppressing them is not the way to do it. There's a high emotional and physical price that comes with holding it all in."

Eddie stood and stepped down the two steps and turned to face Charlie and Nora, "I've seen a lot of people carrying around a lot of pain, but they can't really be themselves or have good relationships because it takes so much energy to keep their pain from coming to the surface."

Eddie smiled at Charlie and Nora. "Well, I better go and finish saying my goodbyes. I probably won't see a lot of these folks again. I hope to see you two next year." He gave a wave and started toward the trail.

"Wait, Eddie! Can you spare a couple more minutes?" Charlie motioned for Eddie to come back to the porch. "There's something I need to tell you."

Charlie's heart was racing, and he gripped the arms of the wooden rocker. "I heard most of your message tonight, and I want to ask a question. You said we need to go back and face our greatest pain, our greatest failures, right?"

Eddie nodded.

"Nora and I," Charlie glanced at Nora's face and started again. "Nora and I have a son that we haven't talked about--Danny."

Nora stopped rocking. Charlie had not spoken Danny's name in public for a long time.

Eddie broke the silence. "How old is your son?"

"He …he was eighteen. He was killed six months ago in an accident." No one moved. The only sound came from the crickets chirping in the night.

Charlie cleared his throat and spoke softly, almost reverently. "He was driving his pickup truck one evening and something happened that caused him to miss a turn. The truck crashed down a ravine; he was killed instantly."

Eddie sat still, looking into the Charlie's face. Even in the poor light, Eddie could see the tears in his eyes.

"I am so sorry, Charlie. I had no idea." There was another long silence, then Eddie finally asked, "And how have you both been doing?"

"It has been…" Charlie searched for the right words, "…rough. It has been really rough."

Eddie nodded silently.

"It was April 4, I had just gotten up to have coffee, as I always did before I met my friends for breakfast. I went out to get the morning paper and I heard some sirens off in the distance. I didn't really think anything of it. It was foggy, and I had a hard time seeing the paper. I found it and went back in and was having my coffee when they knocked at the door. I thought maybe one of the neighbors was having trouble getting his car started, but it was Art and Jerry, two policemen I know. They came in and told me Danny had been in a bad accident."

Charlie could feel his face getting hot. He hesitated, not wanting to repeat out loud the words they had said. Nora put her hand on his arm and Eddie stepped back on the porch and knelt by Charlie's rocking chair, putting his hand on Charlie's knee.

"Jerry told me they were still trying to get Danny's body out of the truck, down at Devil's Elbow, where it happened. I just couldn't believe what they were telling me. So I grabbed the keys and headed out to Devil's Elbow, waded through the water and mud to his truck…to Danny!"

Eddie glanced at Nora. He had never seen such pain on any-one's face.

"When I pulled back the blanket and saw his face...when I saw his face and he didn't answer me, I screamed his name."

Charlie felt a deep, black sorrow rising up from somewhere in-side him. Perspiration was running from his hair and down his face. He shifted in his chair and made the decision to not swallow his sorrow this time.

"I knew he was gone."

Charlie's body shook as he started to cry; this time, he didn't hold back. It started as a whimper but erupted into screams. Eddie and Nora were by his side, holding his shoulders as Charlie's emo-tions came boiling out. For several minutes, Charlie's weeping was intense and heartbreaking.

It was the first time he had openly mourned the loss of his son.

Afterward, Charlie leaned back in his chair, breathing much easier. He took a deep breath, maybe the first deep breath he had taken since he pulled the blanket back from Danny's face that fog-gy morning.

He felt self-conscious, and let out a long sigh. "Thanks for hold-ing onto me...I feel much better now."

Eddie looked at Nora, and they both released their grip.

"I--I'm sorry for causing so much commotion," Charlie whispered.

Eddie smiled. "Charlie, no need to apologize. I think you have just done yourself a big favor. I can tell by looking at your face that you are probably more comfortable with yourself than you have been in a long time."

Nora smiled and nodded. She could see it in Charlie's face too. She excused herself and went inside to get a damp cloth for her husband.

"Charlie, you look like a different person to me," Eddie said. "This is a good example of what I was trying to say in my message earlier tonight. God knows us better than we know ourselves, and the Bible encourages us to bear one another's burdens. When you let me know about Danny just now and talked about your deepest pain with me and Nora, it was as though you allowed us to share this pain with you."

Eddie looked into Charlie's eyes as he spoke. "It seems to me you have been hurting yourself by holding all of this pain inside you."

"Well, I don't think I want to do this every time I talk about Danny."

Eddie understood. "It won't always be like this."

Nora handed Charlie the damp cloth, very aware that Charlie had just experienced an important breakthrough.

Eddie stepped off the porch again. "I need to run along and visit with some of the others before it gets too late." He looked directly at Charlie. "Don't be afraid to face your pain by remembering the time and places where the worst has happened. The only way to get over your pain is to go through it."

Charlie listened and nodded as Eddie disappeared into the darkness.

Charlie and Nora sat quietly on the front porch for several minutes. It was Charlie who broke the silence.

"I feel so much better right now." He let out another long sigh. "I feel I need to apologize for asking you to keep quiet about Danny's death."

Nora's eyes filled with tears as she sat in silence and rocked.

"You know what I miss, Nora? I really miss everyone back home in Ladner."

"So do I."

"I want to go back, but I wasn't sure I could stand the painful memories. After what just happened tonight, I think maybe we should try it."

"I think I would like that, Charlie." She got up and stepped closer to him and kissed him on the cheek. She took his hand as he got up and followed her into the cottage, shutting the door behind them as they turned in for the night.

CHAPTER FORTY-THREE

The next day, mothers and their children carried out their suitcases, preparing to leave. Charlie went to Joe Wright, the camp director, and told him that he and Nora would be leaving soon, ending their time as volunteers. They would be glad to stay until Joe could find a replacement.

Joe said he understood, especially considering Charlie's recent health issues. He had just heard from his uncle saying he was retiring and would love to work as a mechanic at the camp. He hated to lose Charlie but felt the Lord was providing a replacement to work alongside Ralph.

Charlie and Nora stayed at Ridgeview a few more days, long enough to make the doctor appointments and get the all-clear on Charlie's follow-up tests.

Dr. Strickler's parting words to Nora and Charlie were, "Those things we try to suppress usually have a way of coming out....one way or another. Your heart will be much healthier if you can talk about it with someone."

Charlie and Nora felt they wanted to see some of the East Coast before their return to Ladner. Joe knew of their plans and suggested they park their trailer and leave their other things there while they traveled. They could pick up their belongings on the way back to Ladner.

It was Monday, JD's day off, and when the phone rang, JD barked a sharp order to Anna, "Tell whoever it is I'm in the shower." He got out of his chair and walked to the bathroom and stepped in, standing fully clothed in the dry shower stall, so he wouldn't make a liar out of Anna.

Anna used her polite preacher's-wife voice, "This is the parsonage."

"Mom, this is Charlie."

"Oh, Charlie, it's so good to hear your voice. Are you all right?"

When JD heard her say Charlie's name, he was at her side in no time, snatching the phone from her hand.

"Son, is that you?"

Charlie tensed a bit as he responded, "Yes, Dad, it's me."

"Great to hear from you, son. We had a great day yesterday at church. We went over the top in our attendance drive. We hoped to have 500 in Sunday School and…"

"Daddy, Nora and I have decided to come back home to Ladner."

"What?" JD could hardly believe it. "Are you coming back for a visit, or are you really moving back here?"

"We are coming back to stay, Daddy."

"Son, is there something wrong with your heart that you haven't told me about?"

Charlie laughed. "No, Daddy. In fact, my heart feels great. I have been cleared by my doctor. With this new pacemaker and some things I have learned about myself, I'm doing just fine."

JD was ecstatic. "Praise God! When will you get here? We can't wait to see you and Nora!"

"We aren't sure exactly when we'll get there. There are some details to work out. The folks who are renting our house will be leaving earlier than we thought, so we are thinking about arriving there a few days before Christmas and spending that time with you and Mom. Is it possible for us to stay in the spare room at your place until our house is empty and we can move back in?"

"Sure, son, of course! You are more than welcome here--anytime." JD's voice rose with excitement, "We will have a home-coming party for you, and it will be a bigger party than the one for the Prodigal Son! Hallelujah!"

Charlie winced at the Prodigal Son comparison.

"Daddy, since we are already out here near the coast, we think we'll travel a while. We want to see some states we've never visited before, and we'd like to take our time and get some sun in Florida. They've told us we're welcome to leave our stuff stored here while we travel, then we'll swing back by to pick up our things and get on our way back home."

CHAPTER FORTY-FOUR

The following weeks were filled with rest and relaxation. Charlie and Nora soaked up the beauty of the Outer Banks in North Carolina and beautiful Myrtle Beach in South Carolina. The inheritance money made it possible for them to enjoy the pleasures of travel without fear of running out of funds.

When they left Myrtle Beach, they traveled down the coast, taking time to tour St. Simon's Island, just off the Georgia coast. They traveled to Daytona Beach and spent some relaxing time there. Soon they were tanned from leisurely days in the sun. Some days they did nothing but lounge on the beach, listening to the surf. Other days, Charlie visited the Daytona Speedway while Nora shopped. Thanksgiving was just around the corner, and neither of them wanted to be in Ladner for Thanksgiving. Their first Christmas without Danny would be hard enough; they didn't need to be there for Thanksgiving.

Nora's cousin, Jim, and his wife Mary lived in Tampa and had always wanted Charlie and Nora to visit. Two weeks before Thanksgiving, Nora called to see if they could possibly visit over the holiday. Jim and Mary were thrilled to host them, and the time for their arrival was set for Wednesday, the day before Thanksgiving.

The Tuesday before Thanksgiving, the Davises decided to grab a quick hamburger at McDonald's. Looking around the restaurant, all Charlie could see were families with children.

Many of the children were with more mature adults—like grandparents. "I guess this is something we will never get to do. I probably shouldn't say this, but if this is what it means to face my pain--well, I'm already sick of it. I'm not sure I'm going to be very good at it."

Nora reached over and put her hand on Charlie's

"I know, honey. It's painful for me too. Maybe we shouldn't expect too much from ourselves yet."

He took a long sip of his soft drink, then confessed. "I had always looked forward to having a grandchild of our own someday. But now..."

CHAPTER FORTY-FIVE

Mary, true to her reputation, brought out her best for the occasion. The Thanksgiving table was color coordinated to perfection. The bouquet of fresh flowers Jim had bought the day before matched perfectly with the desert rose pattern of the dishes that had been handed down to Mary from her grandmother.

Jim and Mary were fully aware of what Charlie and Nora were facing on their first Thanksgiving without Danny. At first, Mary was very tentative, afraid she might say the wrong thing. However, after a while, everyone seemed to relax, enjoying the meal and their conversation together.

Nora helped clear the table as they looked forward to the dessert Mary had prepared. They were enjoying their pumpkin pie when Nora turned to Mary and pointed to the pattern on her salad plate. "I love these dishes, Mary. How long have you had this set?"

Mary smiled, lifted her coffee cup admiringly as she explained. "My grandmother told me when I was only nine years old that she wanted me to have these dishes. I don't think I've ever said this to anyone else, but I always felt I was her favorite grandchild. So, when she died twenty years ago, this entire set was given to me. She even put it in her will to be sure I got them."

Nora smiled, "I have some dishes that were given to me by my grandmother, but…" Nora stopped. "I have no idea what will happen to them when we're gone."

Charlie flinched as he sipped the hot coffee Mary had just poured. Nora's words hit him hard, and these realities were beginning to sink in for both of them. There was no one to whom they could give their belongings when they were gone; there was no promise of an heir. Another reminder of all they had lost.

Jim set his fork on his empty plate and leaned back in his chair. "Mary and I have had some of those same thoughts. We tried for several years to have a child. Finally, we came to the point where we had to accept the fact it wasn't going to happen. We considered adoption, but after checking into it, we decided we would simply invest our lives into other children."

Jim set his coffee cup down and continued. "I had a long talk with our minister about it and tried to explain the helplessness I felt about not having children. You know what he told me? He said, 'Jim, every man has a strong desire to plant a tree, write a book, or father a child.'"

It was silent around the table, and then Jim spoke again. "I thought about what he said, and it's true. All three of those things should be here after a person is gone: the tree, the book…"

Jim didn't finish the sentence, but they all knew what he was going to say. They sat in silence for a few seconds but it felt like an hour.

After spending the weekend with Jim and Mary Christmas shopping together in Tampa, Charlie and Nora got back on the road. They planned to do a bit more traveling on their southern tour before returning to Asheville where they would pick up their things and drive to Ladner.

If all went well, they would be arriving in Ladner just a few days before Christmas. Charlie knew his mother and dad were expecting them to be there, and he certainly didn't want to disappoint them--especially his dad.

CHAPTER FORTY-SIX

J D ran his long fingers through his gray hair and looked again at the attendance and finance reports from the previous day. His church was in the middle of a six-week fund-raising drive. Each year JD received the dreaded financial goal from his bishop, Dr. Samuel Jones.

JD always resented sending the money to Bishop Jones, because he knew most of the money was used to pay for the administrative salaries of the big-shot executives in the Springfield office. JD could never understand why he was required to pay so much money to that office when his church received so little in return.

There were many needs among his own people. Unemployment was on the rise, and the benevolence fund was nearly drained. However, he always paid what was expected. If anything, JD was loyal to those above him on the ecclesiastical ladder.

This year's goal, though, was going to be difficult to reach. The largest factory in town was closing and Ladner was losing nearly three hundred jobs because of the relocation. The church offerings would be hit hard. That meant JD would have to be more creative as he thought about ways to come up with the money to meet the financial goal.

He had already preached three sermons on "seed faith" and promised the people that if they wanted to prosper, they would need to give more. He explained it was much like planting seeds. The more one plants, the more one reaps. He used scripture from Second Corinthians 9:6 to prove his point. "But this I say, He which soweth sparingly shall reap also sparingly; and he which soweth bountifully shall reap also bountifully."

Even with the heavy emphasis on giving to God, JD knew the offerings would be slim. If something didn't happen soon, he would be several thousand dollars short of reaching the goal. He needed a miracle--and fast.

JD sat alone in his office, looking out across the cemetery next door. He rarely allowed his eyes to wander over to Danny's grave. He couldn't count the times he wished his grandson had been buried somewhere else. It sickened him to see Danny's grave stone, but sometimes his eyes seemed to go there without his consent.

In a flash, he had an inspired thought that could have come only from God above, and JD knew it was his answer to bringing in more money in the coming weeks.

JD was so grateful to God that he leaned back in his chair and lifted his hands high in the air. With tears streaming down his face, he thanked God for that special moment of inspiration.

Ladner had a long history of celebrating Christmas in a big way. Everyone in town decorated their homes and businesses. There were banners across Main Street, ribbons on the street lights, and wreaths on every door. JD had been given an inspiration to make it even more special and to raise money at the same time.

JD had taken Anna to Branson the previous year and remembered that a town close to Branson developed a special drive-through Christmas light show that was spectacular. JD recalled the night he took Anna through the maze of Christmas lights.

At the entrance, an attendant told him to turn off his car lights as they entered the lighted area. Then, they drove slowly from one dazzling light display to another. They were very impressed. There were demonstrations of The Twelve Days of Christmas, We Three Kings, and other Christmas carols represented in the light show. It took several minutes to drive through it, and JD remembered that Anna was spellbound. He couldn't remember her ever being so excited about a Christmas light show. She had exclaimed, "Oh, JD! I so wish we had something like this in Ladner. Everyone in town would love it."

It took several minutes to drive through the displays, and when they came to the end, an attendant, dressed like one of Santa's helpers, stood with a red can in his hand asking for donations.

People loved the light show so much that they were quick to give a generous amount. Anna had been ready to give a twenty-dollar donation. JD quickly talked her down to five dollars. He was sure a display such as that would be a moneymaker. And he knew the exact spot to do it.

CHAPTER FORTY-SEVEN

"The cemetery! Are you out of your mind?" Mickey nearly screamed his objection when he heard JD's proposal. How could anyone think of staging a Christmas display in a cemetery?"

JD and Mickey were having coffee at the Boar's Head when JD presented his idea to Mickey. Everyone in the café heard Mickey's response to JD's proposal. Charlie's buddies, Tom, Al, and Tiny, were at the counter, and they heard it too. They all spun around on their stools to see what the commotion was about.

JD waved his hand in the air. "I knew you would probably have this reaction, but I think it's a real moneymaker, Mick. Think about it a minute. This town is crazy about Christmas. We always have a huge turnout at the tree-lighting ceremony on the town square. If we can put up a big Christmas light display in the cemetery and let the people drive through it, I know the folks will go for it, just like they did down near Branson.

Mickey wasn't convinced. JD knew he had to get Mickey on board before he could move forward. Nothing happened in that cemetery without Mickey's approval.

JD pressed forward with his idea as he set his coffee mug on the table. "Mickey, if we have a religious theme to this and can get just the right lighting display, I'm sure God will bless it. There will be throngs of people driving through your cemetery."

JD could see the wheels turning in Mickey's mind: Free advertising for his funeral home and his cemetery.

"We can arrange for someone to pass out programs at the gate. The brochure will feature your funeral home as one of the main sponsors, Mickey. No doubt, you will pick up a lot of business from this. What do you say?"

Mickey took a sip from his mug. *Maybe it isn't a completely bad idea*, he thought.

Mickey had originally felt it would interfere with his December burials. But then he got to thinking that he historically hadn't had many funerals in December, because dying folks usually held on until after the holidays. He could count on a lot of deaths just after Christmas and New Year's.

"Let me think about it some more and get back to you tomorrow."

JD was excited. He could see Mickey was getting interested, and he was confident Mickey would come around to his way of thinking.

JD was starting to come up with other ideas and possibilities to complement his original theme. "Let the birth of Jesus turn your sadness into Joy!" JD's mind was in overdrive, and the creative juices flowed. If Mickey gave the okay, they would need to move fast!

JD paid for the coffees, then turned and spoke to Charlie's buddies at the counter.

"Did you know Charlie is coming back to Ladner? He and Nora should be home by Christmas."

Tom wheeled around on his stool and said, "Excuse me, Reverend, did I hear you say that Charlie and Nora are coming back to Ladner?"

JD smiled as he buttoned his coat. "Yes, we received word just a few days ago. They promised they would try to be here in time for Christmas!"

The three had heard JD and Mickey discussing the Christmas in the Cemetery idea, so Al spoke up.

"I couldn't help but hear you talking with Mickey about the idea of having a Christmas light show in the cemetery. That sounds like an exciting idea."

Mickey had already left, but JD nodded. "Yes, it is still in the planning stages, but we think it has big possibilities to help raise money for the needy folks here in Ladner.

Al seemed a little excited as he stood and stepped closer to JD. "If you need some help getting it set up, let me know. I've had quite a bit of experience with electricity, and I'd be glad to give a hand if you could use someone like me."

"Yes, yes, I think we will need a lot of help getting this up and running before Christmas."

"As a matter of fact, Reverend," Al said, "I have a cousin who lives in Paola, Kansas, and if I'm not mistaken, he had something like this on his farm at one time. Anyone who drove that way from Kansas City could see it along Highway 169. He's old and feeble, and he can't do it now, but I imagine the light display is still stored in one of his barns."

JD saw this as an answer and stamp of approval from God. "Al, this sounds like God's will. Please call your cousin right away to see if he still has it and ask if he will let us borrow it."

JD left the Boar's Head with his head high and great confidence that his idea was indeed God's will. He could feel it in his bones.

The very next day, JD received Mickey's okay, just as he had hoped. After that, things started happening fast. Al's cousin still had the Christmas displays stored in his barn, and, yes, he would be happy to donate them to the church and the City of Ladner if he could get a receipt from the church. Both Tiny and Tom offered to go with Al to Paola, drag the displays out of the barn, and haul them back to Ladner.

News of the project was spreading around town. At first, most folks thought JD had lost his mind. But, just as Mickey had, the more they thought about it, the more excited they became about Christmas in the Cemetery. Offers to help set up the display were coming from everywhere.

—‡‡—

JD stood at his office window, looking across the parking lot toward the cemetery. He could imagine the whole place ablaze with Christmas lights; Christmas in the Cemetery. People would love it! He thought of another possible theme: Turning Mourning into Joy.

JD felt strongly there should be a live Nativity scene somewhere in the drive-through light show. No Christmas display should be without it. He had it all worked out in his mind.

He would have the Nativity located near the end of the light display and make it the center of attention. People would see Mary, Joseph, the baby Jesus, as well as the shepherds, live animals such as sheep and donkeys, and even the Three Kings. One of the Three Kings could stand on the side of the road with a large can in his hands, asking for donations. Something for the Christ Child!

The King would say to the people in the cars, "We have Frankincense and Myrrh, but we need your help to give him the gold--or cash." No one could say no to baby Jesus! JD knew the whole thing would work best if he used live animals and a few couples who could take shifts portraying Mary and Joseph.

And a live baby Jesus! That would be the icing on the Nativity cake. JD rubbed his chin as he gave a live baby more thought. The weather in Ladner was unpredictable, and nothing could be planned with any assurance of good weather. The baby was likely the biggest challenge, because there hadn't been a new baby born in his church for quite some time.

It needed to be an infant; a toddler wouldn't do. If the people saw a little baby out in the weather on a cold December night as they drove through, they would surely give more money at the end of the Christmas display.

CHAPTER FORTY EIGHT

J D had no way of knowing that the solution to his Baby Jesus problem was about to be solved. On November 23rd in St. Louis, Missouri, a child was born to a young mother named Sandy Peterson. Danny Davis was the baby's father.

To save her family possible embarrassment, Sandy had stayed with her aunt in St. Louis, working as a waitress in a steakhouse. On Thanksgiving Day, she gave birth to a beautiful baby boy, seven pounds, ten ounces.

He was a perfect baby. Sandy looked into the face of her newborn son and gave her baby his father's name--Danny.

The day after she delivered her baby boy, Sandy was holding him in her arms when Aunt Olga walked in. Pulling a chair up close to Sandy's hospital bed, she measured her words carefully.

"He is absolutely beautiful, Sandy, but when are you going to tell your mom and dad about this?"

"I've been thinking about that, I just don't know how to tell them. I can't keep putting them off like I have every time they've wanted to come see me or asked me to come home to visit them."

Olga put her hand on Sandy's arm. "Well, honey, you aren't the first girl who has had to face her family after something like this. I think I can tell you how they will react when they hear the news."

"Do you think they will disown me, or maybe not love my baby?"

"Well, they will be shocked, for sure. It isn't every day your daughter calls you and says, "Hey, guess what you're getting for Christmas this year!""

Sandy didn't laugh.

"But, after they have time to absorb the shock, I think they will be ecstatic." Looking at the baby, she added, "Who wouldn't want to hold *this* beautiful baby boy?" Olga reached over and patted the edge of the soft blanket wrapped around the baby.

"Do you really think so? You don't think they'll be ashamed of me?"

"Oh honey, I know your mom and dad. I think they'll get used to the idea and welcome you and Danny and be the best grandparents ever! I'm not sure, though, about the Davis family—especially that preacher grandfather."

Sandy and Olga silently pondered how JD, the town's living monument to holy virtue, would take it when he found out his own grandson had been sexually active with his girlfriend before marriage.

JD had preached for years against any sort of sexual activity outside of marriage. He had gone into detail about sexually transmitted diseases and how, almost always, the children of single-parent families turned out to be juvenile delinquents. JD took great pride in pointing to his own family--Charlie, Nora, and even Danny--as great examples of doing everything the way it should be done.

Sandy had something else on her mind that loomed even larger than the shame she might experience when her family and Danny's found out about her baby.

Only Sandy knew what happened the night Danny died--the night she told him she was pregnant.

Olga left when visiting hours were over, and Sandy was alone with her sleeping baby. She replayed in her mind the events of the last night she and Danny were together, like it had happened just last night.

The previous night, Danny picked Sandy up in his pickup and they had gone to McDonalds. They decided to eat in the truck, so after going through the drive-through, they took their hamburgers, fries, and drinks and parked the truck in the parking lot so they could be alone.

Sandy remembered the wave of nausea that swept over her as she opened the sack and smelled the food. She quickly opened the door and vomited in the parking lot. Danny was horrified.

She had done the same thing the morning she learned of Danny's death. Everyone thought it was because of the shock. Then, she had felt sick again when she was with Danny's parents making funeral arrangements.

After she had thrown up that night in the truck with Danny, she shut the door and turned to him, nearly crying. "Danny, I'm so scared."

She remembered Danny holding her and asking, "What's wrong with you? Should I take you to the hospital?"

"No, I don't think the hospital can help us. Danny, I think I might be pregnant."

Danny turned white as a sheet. He gripped the steering wheel with one hand and Sandy's hand with the other. "Are you sure?"

She nodded slowly, "I've missed two periods, something I never do. I'm pretty sure."

"My Dad will kill me when he finds out, and my grandfather will never speak to me again."

They talked about what they might do for several hours that night. They could run off and get married, but they had no money and didn't know where they could get any. They both had school to finish, and people would talk--people would know!

Sandy remembered those last moments together when he drove her home and kissed her for the very last time. She could feel the tension in Danny's body as she held him close. They held onto each other for a long time. She remembered what he said to her just before she went in.

"I don't know what we'll do, but I am going to go out by the lake and think about it. I don't want you to worry. I love you, and God will help us find a way." Sandy remembered his face and the way he held his chest as he drove off into the fog that night.

She wondered early-on if Danny drove his truck over the embankment at Devil's Elbow instead of facing his family. But deep in her heart, she knew he would never abandon her by taking his own life.

Surely, she was the one who caused that accident. In order to calm her guilt and honor Danny, she had ordered the small rose bud for Danny's funeral, and she added another small flower for his school locker. Nora had noticed both anonymous rosebuds but there were no notes attached. Only Sandy knew what they meant.

CHAPTER FORTY-NINE

When Al, Tom, and Tiny arrived at the cemetery with the Christmas lights, JD and Mickey met them at the gate. JD, confident God had given him the vision for this Christmas extravaganza, was pumped. He wanted to supervise every detail.

However, there were a few problems to deal with. There were several grave monuments that people would be driving by in order to see the Christmas display. JD counted ten large granite grave stones.

Each one stood between three and five feet high. JD had been giving it a lot of thought. *How can we make this look less like a cemetery and more like a joyous Christmas scene?* Then he had another flash of inspiration.

Mickey was wringing his hands, already having second thoughts when JD wheeled around with a big smile on his face.

"Why don't we have Lilly bring her staff out here and wrap these large monuments in Christmas paper? You know, the kind that is real shiny? She can make huge bows to put on each one, and they will look like huge Christmas gifts by the time she's finished wrapping them."

Lilly owned a very successful flower and gift shop in town. If anyone could make gravestones look like Christmas decorations, it was Lilly.

Mickey looked at JD in disbelief. "You are out of your mind, JD." Mickey delivered that opinion without inflection or facial expression. "The families who own those monuments will sue me if they find out we did something like that."

"I will convince them it's for the greater good." JD walked down the gravel road, took a pen from his pocket, and wrote down the information from each granite block.

"I know all these families. I've even conducted most of these funerals. I will plead with them to let us giftwrap the monuments, at least for a few days. I expect they will go along with it."

Once Mickey and JD finally agreed upon which vacant area would be home to the light display, they approached Tom, Tiny, and Al, who were waiting in the truck. Once they knew where to set up the display, they were out of the truck and ready to get to work. They anticipated it would take about two days to have everything in place, and they were eager to get to it.

And JD was right. The Christmas spirit had taken over in Ladner. The families connected to the grave monuments gave permission to have them giftwrapped. Every one.

CHAPTER FIFTY

Sandy had called her mother to let her know she was coming home for Christmas. When she pulled into the driveway and turned off her car, her heart was pounding.

She unlatched the safety strap on the infant carrier and picked up her sleeping baby boy. Maybe her parents wouldn't be angry once they saw his precious face. She slung the huge diaper bag over her shoulder and walked to the door with the baby bundled in her arms.

It felt strange to knock on the door of her own home, but under the circumstances, she felt she should announce her arrival. Sandy knocked softly on the door, and when no one answered, she knocked again.

She heard footsteps hurrying to the door, and it was pulled opened. Gloria Peterson stood in the doorway and looked into her daughter's face. It had been a long time.

Sandy, feeling self-conscious and not knowing what else to say, said the only thing that came to mind. "Hi, Mom! Merry Christmas!"

When Gloria saw Sandy holding what appeared to be a baby and the diaper bag hanging on her shoulder, she was speechless. Then, after a brief pause, she screamed with excitement. She was overjoyed to see her daughter.

"Sandy, my sweet baby girl. I'm so glad to see you! Welcome home. Whose baby do you have there?"

There was a moment of awkward silence as Gloria waited for an answer. Sandy took a deep breath and held the baby out to her mother.

"Mom, this is your new grandson."

<hr/>

JD was more than pleased with the response to Christmas in the Cemetery!" At first, folks thought it was an outrageous idea, but JD was able to overcome their reluctance by announcing that Santa would be handing out free candy at the gate. He even persuaded Micah to dress up like Santa Claus.

Always looking for a way to witness for the Lord, JD had the candy canes wrapped in bright pieces of paper with a quote from the Bible: "For the wages of sin is death, but the *gift* of God is eternal life."

JD reasoned that the ride through the cemetery might remind them of their own mortality, while the candy could assure them they could live forever by trusting in Jesus--the *gift*! After all, the gift was the point of it all.

JD thought it was a stroke of genius to include that Bible verse on each candy cane.

<hr/>

Two days before Christmas, the parsonage looked like a magazine cover. There was a Christmas tree in nearly every room. Anna wanted to make this a very special Christmas for Charlie and Nora, their first without Danny.

The telephone rang and JD answered, "This is the parsonage."

It was Lilly. In addition to decorating the monuments, JD had asked her to help coordinate the live Nativity scene. She had gladly taken the responsibility. The reason for her call today was about the baby she had lined up to play baby Jesus.

Lilly had arranged for the Michaels baby to be Jesus. However, the baby's mother had called to let Lilly know that the baby had come down with a cold, and she didn't think it was a good idea for him to be outside—at night--in the middle of winter.

Lilly simply didn't know of any other babies, much less babies whose mothers would be willing to let them play baby Jesus. Lilly started making phone calls and had her friends calling friends trying to find an understudy baby.

"Don't worry, Lilly," JD told her, "I'm sure God will help us find a way to get a baby out to the cemetery by tonight. The Lord will provide."

After the phone call, JD told Anna about the predicament. Anna's suggestion was to use someone's play doll.

JD considered that for only a moment, then fired back. "Anna, we have advertised a live Nativity! It would make me look like a liar if we don't have a live baby."

Gloria Peterson, Lilly's friend, had worked for Lilly's floral shop off and on as extra seasonal help, and she was one of the people Lilly called who might know someone who had an infant.

Gloria listened to Lilly's desperate plea and realized the answer to the problem might have just walked through her front door.

"Lilly, I think I might be able to help. Can you give me just a few minutes and let me call you back?"

"Sure, Gloria, if you think you can help, that would be so great. I'll look forward to hearing from you."

Gloria got off the phone and turned to Sandy. "Honey, Ladner is putting on a drive-through Christmas light display that starts tonight. It's set up on the road that goes through the cemetery, and at the end of the display there is going to be a live Nativity with animals and people to play Mary and Joseph and the Wise Men. That was Lilly on the phone just now; she's been helping with the decorating and all. She said the baby they had lined up to be baby Jesus has a cold. I wondered how you would feel about letting little Danny take part in the Nativity tonight."

"Oh, gosh, Mom, I don't know; it's so cold and snowy. Do you think it's a good idea to have him outside that long?"

"I'm sure he'll be okay. He'll be bundled up, and I would be surprised if they didn't have heaters running to keep you warm."

Sandy thought about it. *Maybe it would be fitting for me to hold Danny near his father's grave on his very first Christmas.* The more she thought about it, the more she felt the hand of destiny was on her baby.

Sandy told her mother she would do it under one condition. She would do it only if she could hold her own baby and be Mary. She could *never* contemplate another woman holding baby Danny that close to his father, especially on a snowy Christmas Eve.

Gloria had been thinking too. It occurred to her that the baby who would be playing Jesus was JD's great grandson, but she decided to go ahead and call Lilly back and tell her about Sandy's baby.

When Lilly heard Gloria's news, there was a long silence, and Gloria sensed Lilly's shock.

"Gloria, are you kidding me? You can't be serious."

Gloria allowed herself a small chuckle. "I assure you, Lilly, I couldn't be more serious. Sandy is right here in front of me, holding baby Danny--JD's great grandchild--and he is the cutest thing you ever did see!"

"Well, congratulations, Gloria. I can't wait to meet your grandbaby."

"One more thing," Gloria said. "Sandy said she will need to be Mary; she doesn't want someone else to hold her baby. But with that condition, she is willing to go for it if you want her to do it. What do you think?"

"Well," Lilly said, "JD told me just before I called you that the Lord will provide. So, let's do it. Tell Sandy to bundle up and come on over to my shop. I'll get her dressed in the Mary costume. I'll try to conceal her face behind the folds of material so no one will recognize her."

CHAPTER FIFTY-ONE

It was snowing when Charlie and Nora pulled up in front of the parsonage. Nora breathed a prayer of thanks that they had made it home safely.

Anna and JD were waiting at the door with open arms. Charlie hugged his mother and whispered, "Merry Christmas, Mom," while Nora hugged and greeted JD. Charlie brushed the snow from his hair and started to shake hands with his dad, hesitated, and then hugged JD. "Merry Christmas, Daddy!"

JD was clearly pleased to have his son home, but also detected the sadness in his son's voice. Every Christmas for the last eighteen years, Danny had been with them. No one mentioned it, but they all were thinking of Danny.

Charlie and Nora could not remember a time when Anna's cooking tasted any better. After dessert and coffee, the four of them lingered at the table, watching through the window at the accumulating snow. The cars going by the parsonage seemed to be creeping along, and JD was getting nervous, hoping the snowplows could keep up.

"I have a surprise for you, son," JD said after watching the falling snow for a few minutes. "I didn't tell you this earlier, but the Lord gave me a wonderful idea to raise money for our benevolence fund at the church."

Charlie could see that his dad was excited about it.

"I could tell you more, but I think we'll just show you."

JD looked at Anna and smiled, "Let's leave the dishes for later and go show them now. The roads may get worse, and I sure don't want to get stuck."

They quickly put on their coats and boots and climbed in JD's big Buick. Charlie and Nora were very curious about the special surprise JD had promised.

⇥ ⇤

As JD steered past the church toward the cemetery, Charlie saw the glow of lights in the distance, and then he saw that the glowing lights were in the cemetery and there was a line of cars just up ahead.

The snowflakes were large and beautiful, making the whole scene seem like a fairyland. Anna and Nora couldn't stop talking about how beautiful it was.

JD was praying they wouldn't get stuck. They fell in line with the other cars waiting to turn into the cemetery. JD frowned as he recognized Tom's junk-filled pickup just up ahead of them. Charlie saw it too. It was his breakfast buddies from the Boar's Head.

As the line inched forward, occasionally, someone up ahead would get temporarily stuck, but there were always a few Good Samaritans who jumped out of their cars and got things moving along again. The citizens of Ladner were in the caring spirit of Christmas.

After several minutes of inching along in the snowy procession, they approached the entrance where Micah greeted them in his

Santa suit. "Merry Christmas!" he called out as he moved toward the car.

Micah was covered in snow, but it added to the ambiance. He reached into his bag to give a candy cane to JD through the lowered window. JD frowned as he took the candy, thinking he smelled alcohol on Micah's breath. He quickly raised the window and made a mental note to speak to Micah again about his drinking.

The line of cars moved slowly through the light displays toward the lighted Nativity. Charlie and Nora hadn't been to the cemetery since the day they left Ladner, and Charlie felt himself becoming tense.

The flashing colored lights, enhanced by the falling snow, were made even more impressive by the size of the large snowflakes. Norah and Anna were "oooing" and "ahhhing" at the magnificent light display. The ten granite monuments were beautifully wrapped with colored lights on each one. Lilly and her staff had delivered what JD had requested. One would not guess that this was a cemetery.

At the very end of the display, the Nativity scene was just as JD had envisioned it. Mickey had loaned one of his funeral tents so that most of the Nativity actors were sheltered from the snow. Lilly had arranged bales of hay around the edge so that it didn't resemble a graveside funeral.

Just inside the opening of the tent were colored lights shining on the center of attention: baby Jesus and Mary. Lilly had draped fabric around Sandy's head in such a way that only her eyes were visible. No one would have guessed her identity.

Tom had set up a generator just behind the tent out of sight. The heater was near Mary and the baby. Next to Sandy was Lilly's nineteen-year-old nephew, Paul, who was also dressed with lots of fabric--partly to keep him warm. He stood stiffly nearby, just as he had been instructed.

There were three large sheep and one baby lamb in a nearby pen that was unprotected by the tent. In the heavy snow, all four looked like snowballs. In addition to the sheep, two donkeys were tied up near the front edge of the tent. They were facing the mother and baby.

Following JD's explicit instructions, two shepherds with long staffs stood near the baby. Their shepherd attire also consisted of extra layers to protect them against the cold. Although covered with snow, the Three Kings were stationed near the roadway. The king standing nearest the cars asked for a contribution, exactly as JD had requested.

Above the Nativity was a huge white star that measured two feet long and two feet wide. Al programmed the star to blink, and it was so bright that its glow could be seen from the main road.

Nora and Anna thought the scene resembled a Christmas greeting card. By any standard, it was impressive. Every carload of onlookers stopped to take it all in and meditate on the meaning of the first Christmas. Some tried to take pictures through open car windows, but the snow was so heavy it was practically impossible.

As JD eased his big car near the Nativity scene, he proudly announced to his family, "This is it--this is what it is all about. Praise God!"

The Nativity was on Charlie's side of the car, so JD lowered the windows on that side. He didn't want them to miss anything. He was very proud of his creation.

It was just then that the engine on Tom's truck--just ahead of JD's Buick--died. Tom tried repeatedly to restart it, and behind him, oblivious to the fact that the truck wouldn't start, JD grew more impatient. He flashed his headlights, then tapped his horn. Behind him, others were doing the same.

Tom kept grinding the starter and pumping the accelerator, trying his best to start what JD had once called a pile of junk. The polite tapping of horns turned into long blasts of horn blowing.

The live animals lifted their heads, nervously looking toward the long line of cars.

For a moment, it seemed the old engine might start, but not in the way Tom had hoped for. JD had eased his Buick up right behind the dilapidated truck. He was less than five feet away when the old truck backfired loudly.

Later, people who were just entering the cemetery line would say that it sounded like someone had shot off a canon in the cemetery. The sound startled everyone in the long line, even with their car windows rolled up. There was a bright orange and blue flame that fired from the back of the exhaust pipe on Tom's rust bucket. It blistered the paint on JD's beautiful black Buick. For a brief moment, JD was speechless.

Things went from bad to worse very quickly. The noise, coupled with the fire from the exhaust, startled the animals. As it turned out, it was a mistake to tie the donkeys to the stakes holding up the tent.

When the donkeys heard the backfire, they both reared up on their hind legs and bolted away from the sound, pulling up the stakes that supported a substantial part of the Nativity tent.

It happened so quickly that Sandy hardly had time to react. When she heard the sound of the backfire and saw the fire shooting out of Tom's truck, she, like everyone else, nearly jumped out of her skin. Then, she felt the canvas of the collapsing tent sliding across her head as the donkeys took off across the cemetery, dragging the tent, rope, heater, and stakes behind them.

In the melee, the small fence that enclosed the four sheep was knocked down, and the sheep, frightened, much like the donkeys, also took off across the cemetery in the deep snow.

Joseph, the shepherds, and the kings gave chase, yelling as they ran after the spooked donkeys, forgetting all about the sheep. Sandy sat alone on the remaining bale of hay with a crying baby in her arms--in the falling snow.

All that was left of the original set was the bright star dangling loosely over her head. The star had been anchored to a single pole--the only thing the animals had not dragged away.

"Oh, my God!" JD gripped the steering wheel as the fire flared from Tom's truck. Catastrophe unfolded before his very eyes. Momentarily, everyone in his car sat stunned by the fire and the loud boom.

Then, when they realized they were okay, they saw the donkeys running off with the tent, rope, and stakes dragging behind them. JD pounded the steering wheel with his fist. "Oh, my God! This can't be happening! Oh, Jesus! No, no, no!"

He jumped out of his car and began barking orders to the shepherds and kings. It was too late. The frightened animals were scattered across the cemetery. All JD could hear were the screams of the shepherds, Joseph, and the kings as they gave chase.

Several men had jumped out of their cars when they saw the flash of light and heard the sonic-like boom. People were running in all directions, chasing the animals. The snow was so dense and the visibility so poor that one could see only a few yards ahead. People were yelling to the shepherds, trying to give helpful direction to where the animals had fled.

JD's Christmas in the Cemetery had turned into a nightmare.

Following JD's lead, Charlie also gave chase to some of the sheep that were trying to escape. The three mature sheep headed in a different direction than the lamb. Charlie spotted the struggling lamb. He felt sure he could catch the small animal.

The snow was well over the top of Charlie's boots, but this was not a time to worry about wet feet. He kept his eye on the lamb as it tried running through the deepening snow. Finally, he caught it, shivering, cold, and very scared. When he reached down and picked up the frightened animal and looked around, he realized the lamb was in the vicinity of Danny's grave and near one of the wrapped monuments. With one arm around the lamb, Charlie reached over with his free hand and slowly scooped away the deep snow.

Sure enough, he was at the place that represented his deepest pain. He was still breathing hard and could easily see his own breath. He paused a moment and took a second look. The headlights from the cars helped illuminate the marker. Danny's name was visible. With the lamb in one arm and tears in his eyes, Charlie whispered, "Merry Christmas, son." Then, he gently carried the lamb back toward the car.

With both JD and Charlie out of the car and in the middle of the cemetery chaos, Nora and Anna turned their attention to the Mary, who sat alone on the bale of hay with a crying baby. Sandy kept her baby covered and tried to comfort him.

Nora lowered her window and called out through the falling snow to the helpless mother, "Don't stay out in this weather with your baby! Come, get in here with us where it's warm."

Sandy thought she recognized the voice from the car, but with the heavy snow, the crying baby, and all the loud confusion around her, she didn't know it was Nora.

Nora opened the car door to welcome the approaching mother and baby. When Sandy ducked her head to enter the car and slid into the back seat beside Nora, she looked into the eyes of Nora and nearly panicked! Nora's eyes met hers.

Nora screamed with delight, hugged her, and said, "Oh, Sandy! I had no idea you were Mary!" Anna, still in the front seat, turned around, wide-eyed with disbelief,

"Neither did I. We thought you were still in St. Louis with your aunt."

Sandy was shocked to see Danny's mother and grandmother. Her first instinct was to keep the baby covered. But it was useless; the two older women wanted to see the baby who, by this time, had stopped crying.

Nora was ecstatic, "Oh, Sandy, honey. I can't tell you how wonderful it is to see you. I have thought about you so much and wished we could talk. But, to see you here tonight--well, just seeing you here will make my Christmas complete!" Nora leaned over and hugged Sandy a second time.

"Whose baby is playing baby Jesus? Let me see him."

Sandy, knowing her secret was out, swallowed hard and slowly slipped back the soft blanket revealing the face of her son.

The light from the nearby star was just enough to illuminate the baby's face. When Nora saw it, she looked up into Sandy's eyes and then back to the face of the baby cradled in his mother's arms.

Nora's eyes widened as she placed one hand on Sandy's shoulder and the other on the baby's tiny head, "Oh, Sandy! Is this--"

Sandy nodded.

"He looks--" She couldn't get the words out, so she tried again. "He looks just like Danny."

Anna was on her knees, peering over the front seat. Grandmother and great grandmother looked into the face of their grandchild.

Just then, JD and Charlie opened the car doors, brushed the snow from their boots and started to slide into their seats beside Anna and Nora.

Nearly out of breath, Charlie exclaimed, "I found the little lamb and got it back inside a makeshift pen."

Nora looked up at him as she smiled. "And while you were rescuing one lamb, we found another little lamb you should know about. Merry Christmas, Charlie!"

EPILOGUE

*A*nd so it was that a father's grief found its way home to the unlived *joys and sorrows still to come. Ready to face the future, and carrying the memory of their son in their hearts, Charlie and Nora founded a home for runaway and homeless children in Ladner with the money they inherited.*

JD, his heart softened in old age, could often be seen walking along the cemetery path surrounded by children, as he regaled them with stories.

Micah gave up drinking for good and became a beloved caretaker at the children's home, which was aptly named Danny's Haven.

In time, Sandy married a good man from Ladner, a man who gladly accepted the responsibilities of helping her raise the little boy named Danny.

BOOK CLUB/SMALL GROUP QUESTIONS:

1. Charlie and JD, even though father and son, could not be more different. In what ways do you think JD influences Charlie's personality and attitudes?
2. What do you think of the relationship between Charlie and Nora?
3. What do you think of the relationship between JD and his wife?
4. In what way do you think Ladner represents small town America? What did you especially like about the town?
5. When JD decides that Danny had to die so more people, especially teens, could find their way to membership in the church, what did you think? Was JD earnest, conniving, or both?
6. When JD and Nora leave Ladner, were you glad for them? Did you see them as running away, or having the good sense to withdraw so they could heal?
7. In what ways are Charlie and Nora's grief processes different?
8. Could you understand or relate to Charlie's anger?

9. What did you think of the Bible camp and the insights gained there?
10. Why do you think the young boy who Charlie comforted when they were stranded due to a rain storm had such an impact on Charlie?
11. Talk about losses you have experienced and how you relate to Charlie's journey and his and Nora's many emotions.
12. Do you think Charlie's near heart attack was a wakeup call? What was the hidden gift that it brought?
13. What did you find hilarious about the outrageous idea of the *Christmas in the Cemetery*? What does returning home mean to you?
14. Did the ending surprise you or did you see it coming? Do you think joy and sorrow can co-exist?
15. In what way has this novel inspired you?

Dear Reader,

My wife and I were sitting in our favorite Mexican restaurant, eating chips and salsa, when our friend, Harold Ivan Smith handed me the copy of an article written by a man who accepted the challenge of writing an entire novel during the month of November. The article referenced a website: http://nanowrimo.org/

Even though this website was originally formed to encourage young writers, there was something about it that caused me to take up the challenge too. Could I really crank out fifty thousand words during the month of November? I decided to go for it and actually came out with over sixty thousand words. I wrote this book in one month but have been revising and re-writing over the past six years. I hope you have enjoyed reading this book as much as I enjoyed writing it.

Finally, on January 12, 2012 a small part of our painful story was aired on National Public Radio & Storycorps.org. It is 3 minutes long but tells of our journey.

Dennis' email: firstof1019@gmail.com

Twitter: @hoosierrunner

Website: www.thewritingapple.com

Made in the USA
Charleston, SC
24 June 2016